Praise for
A Pup Called Trouble

★ "An enthralling adventure with emotional heft
and read-aloud potential."
—ALA *Booklist* (starred review)

"A fast-paced, immersive exploration of urban wildlife
from a satisfying animal point of view."
—*Kirkus Reviews*

"Based on real-life instances of coyotes inhabiting
Central Park, Pyron's tale deftly navigates the animal
adventure genre with a lively voice.
Readers will be captivated."
—*School Library Journal*

"A sweet tale about something we all yearn for,
whether we're four footed or two footed: friendship and
a place to call home."
—Suzanne Selfors, bestselling author

BOBBIE PYRON

A Pup Called
Trouble

KATHERINE TEGEN BOOKS
An Imprint of HarperCollins Publishers

Katherine Tegen Books is an imprint of HarperCollins Publishers.

A Pup Called Trouble
Copyright © 2018 by Bobbie Pyron

Library of Congress Control Number: 2017949558
ISBN 978-0-06-268523-0

Typography by Andrea Vandergrift
19 20 21 22 23   PC/BRR   10 9 8 7 6 5 4 3 2 1
❖
First paperback edition, 2019

For Charlene:
moon sister, coyote and opossum lover,
always up for an adventure

A Pup Called
Trouble

1

Eyes Wide Open

On an early spring day, in a den tucked beneath the roots of an old oak tree, four coyote pups were born.

During the first week, they nursed and slept just like all newborn puppies do.

All except one.

Unlike the other pups, one member of the Singing Creek Pack was born with eyes wide open and ears— no bigger than thumbnails—twitching with curiosity.

He heard the *shhh, shhh, shhh* of the wind wandering in the trees. He turned toward the *caw! caw!* of a crow. His blue eyes widened. Light! Light dappled by leaves danced above and beyond.

With a tiny squeak of excitement, the coyote pup

left the warmth of his sleeping mother's side. He scrabbled and stumbled on wobbly legs across the cool dirt floor of the den and up the tunnel toward the light.

With one last scramble, the little pup pulled himself up and emerged, blinking, from the den. He sat on his fat rump and lifted his tiny nose to the air. So many scents! Not his mother's deep, comforting musk or the milky sweetness of his brother and sisters or the rich, dark smell of the earth.

Here was the scent of green leaves just unfurling, the sap rising in the trees. Here, the air was rich with the smell of feathers, fur, tiny green shoots pushing up through wet ground and the last pools of snow.

He stood and turned his ears toward a sound: a faint rustling in the grass. He wiggled his nose. Something warm and furry scratched in the dirt. The little coyote trembled with barely contained excitement. Although the pup was only days old, thousands of years of coyote instinct coursed through his veins. He was, after all, a hunter.

The pup took one step and then another out into the sunlight. He closed his eyes against the unaccustomed bright, so he did not see the great, wide form of an eagle flying low across the meadow.

But he did hear the bloodcurdling hunting cry of the bird.

The pup squealed in fear. He turned to run back to the safety of the den.

He felt the *swoosh* of the enormous bird's wings. He looked up into fierce, hungry eyes, something he would never forget. The pup pressed his belly against the ground as the eagle hurtled toward him.

"No!" came an angry bark.

The pup's father hurled himself between his son and the eagle. The eagle's outstretched talons scraped across the shoulders of the larger coyote.

The pup watched in amazement as his father wheeled and, with barely the flick of an ear, leaped up and grabbed the eagle by the tail feathers.

The eagle screamed in outrage. With one mighty beat of his wings, he pulled free of the coyote and climbed into the sky.

Father coyote sniffed his son from tip to tail. Satisfied that he was unhurt, he gently nipped the small pup. "What in the name of Mother Moon are you doing out here?"

The pup was too young, life too new, to explain what drew him from the safety of his mother's side. He looked up and up into his father's yellow eyes and simply said, "I wanted to see."

The father snorted. He picked up his son by the scruff of his neck and carried him down into the den.

Mother coyote woke at the sound of paws on the dirt. She leaped to her feet. With one bound, she grabbed the pup from her mate and carried him back to his mewling brother and sisters.

Father plopped down with a sigh.

Mother sniffed her little wanderer. "I knew when this one was born with his eyes open," she said, tucking him firmly under her paws, "he was going to be all kinds of trouble."

2

Swift, Pounce, and Star

The moon rose twelve nights and the days grew warmer. Finally, the coyote pups climbed from the dark safety of the den, out into the world. They looked about with wonder.

Ferns unfurled toward the sunlight. Frogs sang their welcome to the warmth.

Twist, a yearling from last year's litter, quivered with excitement. He sniffed each pup. "Oh," he sighed. "They are practically perfect in every way!"

"Yes," Father agreed, lying in the sun beside Mother. "Two boys and two girls. Can't do any better than that."

"What shall we name them?" Twist asked.

"Give them time." Mother watched her pups from the top of a sun-warmed rock. "They'll tell us their names.

"In the meantime," she said, "that one is going to keep us busy." She pointed her nose at the pup who'd been born with his eyes open. The pup, who'd followed his curiosity dangerously close to the edge of the creek, now teetered on a slippery stone.

Twist rushed over, grabbed the pup by the scruff of his neck, and brought him back to his mother.

"Maybe he's telling us his name is Curious," Twist said. "Or Wanderer."

As the days passed, the pups revealed their names.

The largest of the pups soon proved the best hunter of grasshoppers and frogs and mice. He was named Pounce.

His long-legged sister could outrun them all when they raced across the wide, green meadow. She was named Swift.

The sister the color of moonlight had the most beautiful voice when the pack sang to the moon at night. Her voice soared all the way up to the stars, so she was named Star.

But as three pups delighted their parents and older brother with their pounce and speed and soaring song, the fourth pup worried them. He displayed an abundance of curiosity and an alarming lack of caution. He was given to wandering and exploring and poking his nose into places where it didn't belong.

Like hornets' nests.

Yowwwwwwwwww!

The young pup tore across the meadow, an angry cloud of buzzing hornets in pursuit.

Twist tenderly licked the pup's swollen snout. The pup winced as the rough tongue stroked his burning nose.

"I just wanted to see what they were doing in there," the pup whimpered.

Mother shook her head, not for the first time.

"What next?" Father wondered aloud.

He didn't have long to wait for the answer.

3

Trouble

Two days later, on a particularly warm day, the Singing Creek Pack napped together in the deep shade of an evergreen tree.

All except one.

The curious pup's ears swiveled one way and then the other. The air pulsed with sounds of spring in the forest: the faint rustle of mice tunneling beneath the grass, the lazy hum of bees, the call of one bird to another, and always, the never-ending song of Singing Creek.

The warm breeze brought a deliciously unfamiliar smell to the young coyote. He wriggled his wet nose trying to sort out this new scent. It smelled green like the grass in the meadow but also like deep, rich earth.

There were far too many interesting things happening in the world to take a nap.

He squirmed from beneath Twist's paw and scooted under the tree branches, out into the bright sun.

I'll just see what there is to see over by that big rock.

He heard a chirp and an angry *chit chit chit* from a small burrow beneath the rock. The curious coyote cocked his head to one side, then pawed at the burrow entrance. "Who's there?" he asked.

"Go away!" a voice snapped.

"Why?" The pup pawed at the opening with both feet.

A squirrel shot out of the hole, between the coyote's front paws, and across the clearing.

"Wait!" the pup yipped. He galloped after the squirrel on his fat little legs. "Wait for me!"

By the time he crossed the clearing, the squirrel was gone. The pup sat on his rump and looked around. Here there was no Singing Creek, no den beneath the roots of an old oak tree.

Here trees were twisted by the wind, their knobby roots clawing sand and stone. Here, rather than lush ferns carpeting the forest floor, the pup's feet rested on rough stones.

The little coyote quivered with excitement. It was

all so strange and new! This was a place beyond where he'd ever been.

His heart raced. He looked back over his shoulder. Surely his family was just a howl away.

Chit! Chit! Chit! Chit!

"There you are," the coyote yipped.

The squirrel angrily flicked its tail and dashed across the stones, then dropped out of sight, the pup in hot pursuit . . .

until he too dropped out of sight . . .

over a rock outcropping . . .

landing with a *plop* on a narrow ledge below.

The pup was in a bit of a pickle. He could not go up and could not go down, nor sideways even.

He whimpered. Where was his mother? Where were his father and his big brother?

The coyote pointed his muzzle to the sky and howled long and high—a howl that ended with three urgent *yip yip yip*s. A howl that said "Help! Help! Help!"

The coyote cocked his ears and listened for an answer. Nothing.

He tried again. *Awwooooooooooooooooo, yip! Yip! Yip!*

Still, no answer.

"Hey," a voice called from above. "What's all the racket?"

A silver face with a black mask of fur peered over the ledge.

The pup blinked. "Who are you?"

A raccoon never answers a question. Instead, he said, "Don't you know some of us are trying to sleep?"

"I'm stuck," the pup whimpered. "And I don't know where I am," he added with a wet sniff.

"And what am I supposed to do about it?" the raccoon muttered. He eyed the coyote pup. "It's not like your clan and mine are friends."

"You won't help me?" the pup asked in a tiny voice.

The raccoon yawned, turned his back to the coyote, and disappeared from sight.

Yip, yip, yip, yap, yap, arowwwwwwwwooooo!

Under the napping tree, Mother sprang to her feet.

Father sat up and shook the sleep from his head. "What was that?"

"A pup in trouble," Mother said.

The three coyotes looked at the three sleeping pups—Pounce, Swift, and Star—and then at one another.

"Uh-oh," Twist said.

"My baby!" Mother cried.

"Here we go again." Father sighed.

Yip, yip, yip, yap, yap, arowwwwwwwwoooo!

The raccoon groaned. It was no use.

He leaned over the edge of the outcropping. "Quiet!"

The pup stopped his howls.

The raccoon rubbed his ears. "You have a voice that could wake a bat."

He sighed. "I guess the only way I'm going to get any sleep is to get you up here."

"Oh, would you?" the pup squeaked hopefully. He shifted nervously on the ledge, his tail tucked between his trembling legs.

The raccoon glared at the pup. "I'll pull you out, but then you're on your own."

He waddled over to a scrubby bush, broke off a branch, and carried it back to the ledge. He eyed the distance between himself and the coyote. It would do.

The raccoon stretched out on his belly. "I'm going to lower this branch down to you. Grab on with those teeth of yours, and I'll pull you up."

The pup did.

The raccoon dug his back legs into the dirt and pulled with all his might.

To the pup's relief, his feet slowly lifted off the ledge.

"Don't let go," said the raccoon.

With a squeak, the pup popped up over the ledge to safety. Both the raccoon and the coyote pup sat on the ground, panting. The raccoon looked over at the ball of fur. "You're an awful lot of trouble for just a pup," he said.

Just then, Mother coyote bounded into the clearing, Father and Twist following close on her heels. She skidded to a halt and looked in horror at her little coyote baby leaning against a large, disreputable-looking raccoon.

"Get away from my child!" she growled.

The raccoon stood and shook himself wearily. "Gladly," he said.

The pup scampered over to his parents, yipping and licking their faces with joy.

"If you've done anything to harm my precious boy, I'll—" Mother said as her nose searched every inch of the pup's body.

"Lady," the raccoon said as he ambled off, "I wish you luck. That one there, he's trouble."

And from that day forth, the pup was called Trouble.

4

The Makers

Mother and Father watched from the shade as their four pups chased Twist around and around the meadow. The gentle hum of bees filled the air. The sweet smell of clover drifted on the breeze.

"It seems Trouble has learned his lesson," Father said. "He's been sticking close to home the last ten moonrises."

And indeed, it was true. Trouble had watched attentively as Mother demonstrated the finer points of stalking voles, mice, and grasshoppers. He had even become almost as fine a pouncer as his brother and gave his sister Swift a good run for her money.

Mother watched Trouble and Twist play tug-of-war with a strip of deer hide. She hoped Trouble had learned his lesson, but she doubted it.

She stood and shook off her uncertainty. "Time to teach them about the Makers," she announced.

"Pups," she barked. "Come!"

The pups lined up behind their parents, with their older brother bringing up the rear. "Now, my pupletts," Father said, "before we start out, what is the most important rule of the Coyote Clan?"

"I know! I know!" Swift yipped. "Never leave a pack member behind."

"That's right," their mother said. "We're family. We stick together, no matter what. We're going farther than you've been before, so stay close."

Trouble's heart quickened. Farther! They were going farther than they had been before. What a delicious idea!

Trouble trotted across the meadow a few tail-lengths behind his brother; his head swiveled this way and that to see all there was to see. They crossed another creek and then another—creeks that did not sing in the same musical way his creek did. For just a moment Trouble hesitated, then hurried to catch up with his family.

They skirted the remains of a tumbledown shack

rich with the scent of rodents. The lingering sweet aroma of hope and the bitter smell of loss clung to the rotting wood walls.

Trouble stopped to sniff a rusted bucket. The rust smelled sharp, like cold spring water, but there, just there, he caught a salty whiff that both worried and fascinated the pup.

Twist nudged him from behind. "Keep moving, puplett," he barked.

"But—"

The larger coyote nudged him, harder this time. "*Now,* Trouble."

Single file, they wove their way through an old apple orchard laced with the scent of deer and raccoons.

On the edge of the orchard, Mother stopped. "Listen," she said.

The pups threw their large ears forward. In the distance they heard a low, deep growl.

"What is it?" Pounce asked his father in alarm.

Swift readied herself to flee at a moment's notice, and Star shivered and shook next to Twist.

"It sounds *huge*," Trouble exclaimed. "It sounds exciting! Can we go see?"

Mother and Father exchanged a look—one that said that their son had not, in fact, learned his lesson.

Mother nodded. "Yes, we will go see, but you must

promise me something," she said, looking sternly into Trouble's eyes.

"You must promise me you will stay behind me and your father."

His muscles quivered with excitement. He wanted so very much to run faster than he'd ever run toward whatever made that sound, to see what there was to see, and—

"Trouble!" his mother growled. "Do you promise?"

"Yes, Mother," Trouble promised.

The pack worked its way along the edge of the apple orchard, keeping always to the shadows.

Mother stopped. "Do exactly as I do and don't make a sound," she whispered.

She dropped low and slunk through the long grass and weeds. The closer they came to the field, the louder the strange noise grew. Swift growled nervously.

"I want to go home," Pounce whimpered.

Trouble bounced as high as he could—up, down, up, down—to see above the grass.

His father's paw pinned him to the ground. "Stop, or we'll be seen," he hissed.

When they got so close the earth itself began to shake, it was too much for young Pounce. With a squeal, he wheeled and ran for the safety of the trees.

"Go," Father said to Twist, "and stay with him."

Slowly, oh so slowly, five pairs of ears rose above the grass. Five pointed noses worked the air for scents.

Three pair of blue eyes widened in fear and astonishment at the sight before them: a huge, growling beast with green skin that shone in the sun lumbered slowly in the field. Its round feet rolled over and over through the dirt. And atop that huge beast perched a much smaller creature.

"What, what is that?" stammered Swift.

"And why does it allow that small creature to ride on its back?" Star wondered.

Trouble for once was speechless. Not only was this creature huge and shiny, with feet as round and big as the sun, its tail was wide and clawed. And those claws ripped into the earth.

"The beast was made by that creature," Father explained. "So it must do its bidding."

The young coyotes watched as the beast slowly turned and came back the way it had come.

"The creature who made that beast must be very clever," Trouble said with admiration. "And it must be brave and mighty to command this thing."

"The beast is very slow, though," Swift pointed out disdainfully. "It could never run down a rabbit."

"Oh, they are indeed clever," Father allowed. "But

their cleverness is also a source of danger to the Furred and the Feathered."

"To what clan does the small creature belong?" Star asked.

"That," their mother said, pointing her nose, "is a member of the Maker Clan, the most fearsome clan to walk the earth. A clan to be avoided at *all costs*."

The Maker and its Beast moved closer to the edge of the field where the coyotes hid. The sun was above the trees now. A cloud of dust trailed the Beast's clawed tail.

"I don't think the Makers are so terrible," Trouble said, not taking his eyes from the small creature guiding the Beast.

Trouble had never in his short life seen anything so fascinating and confusing. The Maker was small and did not have large teeth or claws of its own. And its smell was not menacing, just salty and a little bit fishy.

"They are worse than terrible," their mother snapped in such a harsh voice that the pups flinched. Trouble tucked his tail. "They are the enemy of the Coyote Clan."

"Come," Mother commanded. She wheeled and slipped back through the tall grass and into the wild woods, her pack following close behind.

All except Trouble. He took one last look at the

wonders in the field, then hurried to catch up with his family.

That night, the pack watched the great, round moon rise above the trees. Even though it was the fourth full moon the pups had seen, they watched it in wonder.

Trouble lay curled against Twist. He felt his brother's heart beat against his back, steady and true. His warm musk surrounded the pup and comforted him.

He thought about all the astonishing things they had seen that day—the old apple orchard; the rusted bucket; the giant, gleaming Beast and the Maker perched on top. What more was out there to see, beyond Singing Creek and their meadow? His whiskers twitched with possibilities. His paws danced with barely contained excitement.

"Mother," Trouble asked, "are there more Makers than the one we saw today?"

"Yes," she replied. "There are many, many Makers. There are possibly more Makers in their clan than coyotes in the Coyote Clan."

Trouble leaped to his feet. He raced in circles of excitement. "Can we go see more tomorrow?"

"No," she snapped. "Nothing good comes from Makers."

Swift shivered with fright. Pounce moved closer to his father, and Star trembled.

Trouble's eyes glowed with dreamy curiosity.

All the pup had heard was the word "more."

And that was just what he wanted. He wanted to see more beyond his home along Singing Creek.

5

The Plan

Summer marched along as summers do. The days grew longer, the air wet and hot. Berries ripened in the sun.

The pups grew as all youngsters do. Stubby legs stretched long as the tall grass, blue eyes turned amber yellow, and baby fluff gave way to rich, tawny coats and bushy tails.

Each day Trouble wandered farther and farther from the den under the old oak tree to see what there was to see.

Beyond the meadow.

Beyond the apple orchard.

Beyond the Maker's field where the giant, shining Beast had lumbered.

Until one day he discovered where the Maker lived.

"Moon and stars," he murmured as his eyes took in all the things the Maker had made: a big aboveground den, a little aboveground den, and all manner and size of shining Beasts scattered, sleeping, in the yard.

He watched with an abundance of curiosity as the Maker came and went from his cave. He wondered at how strangely yet easily the Maker moved about on two legs.

And following the Maker everywhere was a four-legged who looked and smelled in some ways like a coyote but not quite. This animal smelled too sweet, moved too slow to be a coyote. Trouble watched, puzzled, as this creature—clearly an adult—begged like a pup at the Maker's feet.

The afternoon slipped by as Trouble watched and listened and smelled everything he could from his hiding spot. Before he knew it, the sun was slipping behind the forest to the west. He heard a faint *yip yip yowwwwwl!!!*

"Uh-oh," Trouble said, twisting his ears in the direction of the apple orchard.

With one last look at the Maker's den, Trouble slunk through the hedges and past the vegetable garden and toolshed and hightailed it across the field to the old apple orchard.

Twist waited for him in the shade. "Where have

you been?" he barked. "Mother has been calling and calling for you."

"Oh, Twist," Trouble panted with excitement, "I have found more Makers! Did you know there is more than just one Maker?"

"Of course I know there is more than just one Maker," Twist huffed. "There are lots of Makers, just like our mother said."

"More than our pack and the Stoney Ridge Pack put together?" Trouble knew about the Stoney Ridge Pack because his aunt Tip lived with them, and sometimes when the moon was especially full and bright, they all joined together to sing and share stories.

The older coyote gazed beyond the wide field. "Yes, more than the two packs put together. That place you saw, that is just the beginning."

"And brother," Trouble asked as questions tumbled around his mind, "what is that four-legged creature who lives with the Maker?"

Twist snorted. "That," he said with disdain, "is a dog. It is hardly worthy of the Furred Clan."

Before Trouble could ask his next question, Twist shoved him with his shoulder. "Enough of this," he snapped. "We need to get home. Mother is very worried."

"But," Trouble whined.

"*Now,* puplett," his brother growled. "And don't go back to that Maker's home again. No good can come of it."

But of course he did. How could he not? Twist had said this Maker's home was only the beginning.

Day after day, Trouble returned to the Maker's house. Soon, he noticed a pattern: early most mornings, either the male Maker or female Maker carried boxes and bundles right into the belly of a large silver Beast. Then they would crawl inside the head of the Beast; the Beast would rumble to life and dash away down a long road and out of sight. Then, just before the moon rose above the trees, the Beast and the Makers returned.

Trouble, of course, found this all very curious. Where did the Beast and the Makers go? What were they putting in the belly of the Beast? And why did they always come back the same day?

The next morning, Trouble tried his best to follow the Beast, keeping always to the woods. But the Beast was too fast and went too far.

He returned home exhausted.

But still very curious.

Three mornings later, he and his family woke to a steady, cold rain.

"A good day to tidy up the den," his father said.

"Good day to hunt rabbits," his mother said. Pounce, Swift, Star, and Twist agreed.

Trouble decided it was a good day to make a plan. He thought and he thought as the rain poured down. He thought some more as he helped his father widen the den.

By the time the pack gathered that night to serenade the moon, Trouble knew exactly what he was going to do.

6

Stowaway

The next morning, Trouble crawled from the den earlier than usual. The rain from the day before was gone, replaced by thick fog. Barely visible in the southern sky rested the full moon.

He could just make out the sleeping forms of his mother and father lying close together beneath the wide branches of an evergreen tree. And there, beneath a rock outcropping, slept Twist. His chin rested on the strip of deer hide he and Trouble had played with the night before.

For one heartbeat Trouble questioned what he was about to do. Oh, how he loved his family and the den and the ancient oak and the meadow and the creek.

But yet. And yet . . .

Trouble wheeled and slipped away into the fog.

"It's no big deal," Trouble told himself for the tenth time as he made his way to the Maker's house. "I'll see what there is to see and be home by moonrise."

His stomach quivered with excitement and trepidation as he reached the edge of the Maker's field. "They won't even know I've been gone," he assured himself.

Although fog lay thick and low across the field, Trouble knew as soon as the sun came up, the fog would burn off. He fairly flew across the field, then slunk past the vegetable garden, chicken coop, and toolshed.

There it stood: the silver Beast. Trouble's pulse quickened. He raised his nose and sniffed for any scent of Makers or the dog.

None.

He swiveled his large ears and listened for sounds coming from the house.

None.

The back of the Beast was open. The fog was lifting.

A chicken clucked. A crow called out in the field. Somewhere, the Maker's dog barked.

"It's now or never," Trouble said.

With one last look at the house and the wild forest

beyond the fields, Trouble leaped into the Beast.

His heart pounded. His feet skittered and scrambled on the metal floor. He shivered just a bit with the enormity of it all.

Trouble's nose explored his surroundings. He smelled dirt and plants very similar to what grew in the meadow beside Singing Creek. He smelled plump berries and green beans still warm from the sun. His stomach growled. He tipped over a carton of each and gobbled them up.

He heard a door slam. Voices coming toward him.

Trouble scrambled to the back and burrowed beneath a pile of burlap sacks.

"You sure you don't want me to drive into the city today?" a male voice asked. "That fog's thick as pea soup out there."

"Nah," a female voice said. "It'll burn off before you know it. Just help me load the last of the eggs and onions. Our eggs are a big seller at the farmers' market."

Trouble felt the Beast bounce. He heard footsteps walking to the back where he was hidden. He tried his best not to tremble.

A voice right next to him said, "Dang it, how did these cartons get knocked over?"

"Raccoons probably," the other voice answered.

Something thumped down onto the floor, right beside Trouble's head. The smell was sharp and sweet. *Thump, thump, thump.* More sacks of onions piled around Trouble.

"I think that's it," the female voice said. "I'm going to hit the road."

Trouble heard the Makers walk away, felt the truck bounce again.

Just as the coyote inched his head from beneath the cover of the burlap sacks, a deafening rattle and clang took away the light.

All the light. Every bit of it.

Then a loud, low growl rumbled to life beneath Trouble's feet. It grew louder and louder, shaking the floor and the walls and the ceiling of the shelter. Then, to Trouble's horror, the Beast lurched to life. It swung one way, then another, tossing the pup off his feet. He felt the whole of his being vibrating and swaying. He heard the growling and groaning beneath him.

His heart pounded with terror. He burrowed as far as he could beneath the burlap sacks and prayed to Mother Moon that he would somehow find his way out of the Beast.

7

Forest of Stone

A clatter woke the little coyote nestled beneath a warm bundle. At first he thought he slept safe and sound in a pile with his brother and sisters. He smelled the comforting scent of dirt and the sharp smell of green, growing things. His stomach twisted and complained. He was so hungry!

Just as he started to stand, he felt a bounce and heard footsteps.

Trouble froze. He remembered where he was: in the belly of a Beast.

"Let's see what we can unload first," a musical voice said. Hands grabbed boxes of eggs and handed them to another, bigger, Maker.

Trouble burrowed deeper beneath the burlap sacks and tried to make himself as small as possible.

The female Maker handed out crates of green beans, tomatoes, peas, blackberries, and strawberries.

She hefted a bag of yellow onions to her chest. The bottom of the bag split. Onions rolled onto the floor of the truck.

"Dang it," she muttered. "Hang on while I grab a sack and bag them up."

A gloved hand reached down, grabbed for a sack, and, instead, got a handful of Trouble.

Yip!

"Yikes!"

The pup froze. His heart hammered against his ribs. The Maker loomed so close, so large above him. Should he warn the Maker away with a growl and flash of teeth, or should he run?

The Maker took one step toward him.

Trouble bolted between the Maker's legs, leaped past the bigger Maker, and dashed out into the sunlight.

"What is that?" someone cried.

"It's a wolf!" another someone answered.

"It's a dog," someone else said.

Trouble cowered against the stone wall, yellow eyes darting everywhere, looking for a place to escape. Never had he seen so many Makers. Big Makers, small Makers, young and old Makers.

The woman from the truck shook her head. "That," she said, pointing at Trouble, "is a coyote."

A clamor rose from the crowd gathered in the street.

"Get it!"

"Take a picture!"

"Call the police!"

Someone grabbed a large onion and threw it at the cowering pup.

Trouble leaped to his feet, spun in circles looking for the cover of forest, trees, bushes, anything where he could hide. Nothing. Everything was hard. Solid. Unforgiving.

There was only one way to go. Makers screamed and scattered as Trouble dashed straight through the crowd.

The coyote raced blindly forward and careened around a corner. Small Beasts squealed and made the most horrible honking sound. The world spun.

Trouble ducked behind a tall stone den. He swiveled his ears, listening for footsteps, shouts, screams, the bleating of those Beasts. He heard them still, but not so close now.

He looked up. Where was the sky he knew so well? This stone forest rose so high it cut the wide blue expanse to wedges and slivers of white.

"This isn't exactly what I expected," he whimpered.

He smelled food. His stomach growled.

He sniffed a round, shiny thing. Yes, he was sure it contained food.

Trouble stood on his back legs and nosed the lid. It fell with a clatter to the pavement. Right on top, a hunk of something warm and salty smelling. Trouble lunged for the bread, knocking over the garbage can.

Food! Trouble had never seen so much food, and so many different kinds! Vegetables, chunks of meat, chicken bones, and many things he had not smelled before.

The pup wolfed down the meat and had just started in on the remains of a fried chicken dinner when a door swung open.

A huge Maker loomed over Trouble. The sharp smell of anger poured from him. In his hand he clutched a large stick.

The Maker looked at the coyote.

Trouble looked at the Maker, a drumstick still clutched in his jaws.

The Maker roared with fury and raised the stick. "Get out of there!"

Trouble dropped the chicken and hightailed it back onto the street, into New York City.

8

Mischief

The crow sat atop a power pole and fluffed his feathers. He wiped his ebony bill against the wooden pole as he watched for something interesting to happen below.

It is the nature of crows to watch for something curious, something to entertain them. This crow in particular, known among the Furred and Feathered of the city as Mischief, had an endless, bottomless fascination with everything below his wings: cars, windows, humans, crooked things, furred things, paper things, shiny things, and most especially things he could tease.

Mischief watched as vendors set up their booths

for the Wednesday morning farmers' market. Some sold meat; others sold breads; others flowers, fresh vegetables and fruit, eggs, cheeses, and goat's milk. For a crow as curious as Mischief, the farmers' market provided endless possibilities.

Mischief waited in anticipation as one particular truck pulled up. He knew this truck came from far away, out in the country, and always had interesting, tasty things inside.

The driver hopped down from the cab, yawned, and stretched. She rubbed the small of her back and called out a hello to another driver. She strode to the back of the truck, raised the door, and climbed in.

A yip and a yowl and a scream. Something light brown and furry shot from the back of the truck like a cannonball.

Mischief swooped down and perched on the side mirror of a truck for a closer look.

"Well, well, well, if it isn't a member of the Coyote Clan," the crow said. "This ought to be rich."

Mischief watched with delight as the humans shouted and waved their arms and ran about like panic-stricken pigeons, as they were prone to do when faced with something unfamiliar.

"Get it!"

"Leave it alone!"

"Call the police!"

An onion bounced off the young coyote's tawny side. Trouble bolted through the crowd and tore across the square and out into the street.

Mischief lifted into the sky and followed.

The crow watched the pup race into the road. Horns blew; a taxi swerved to miss the coyote and slammed into another taxi.

"Oh ho," Mischief cawed with delight.

He followed the coyote as it raced in a panic one way and then another, until it ducked into a dark side street.

When the coyote pulled the trash can over, Mischief knew exactly what would come next.

"You have a lot to learn," the crow called to the coyote as it raced down the sidewalk, Mischief following overhead.

9

Around the Next Corner

Trouble panted from beneath the cover of low bushes lining the front of yet another of the towering stone places that smelled of Makers.

He knew he should return to the place where he had left the Beast and sneak back inside. He lifted his nose and sniffed. Yes, he was pretty sure he knew the way. That would be the sensible thing to do.

On the other hand, morning sunlight was just now creeping above the tops of the stone spires. The day was young. Surely he could explore just a little farther. After all, the Maker wouldn't leave for home until the sun was low.

Trouble crept from beneath the bushes. He looked

right, then looked left. The path was empty.

He breathed a sigh of relief and shook the worry from his coat. "I'll just see what's around the next bend," he said to no one in particular, and trotted off down the street and around the corner.

And the next one, and the next. Here, on the side of a metal box, the smell of an old male dog; there the sound of something sweet and high like the voice of his sister Star. A gentle gust of wind brought the ancient smell of fish and salt water.

A stronger gust blew a newspaper down the sidewalk. Trouble crouched, then pounced. The wind tore the paper from beneath his paws. With a gleeful yip, Trouble chased the newspaper down the street and around yet another corner until . . .

The wide pathways became busier. Trouble abandoned his chase and took in his surroundings. Nothing smelled familiar. A fine grit filled his delicate nose. He sneezed, then tipped his head back and back as he looked up at the canyons and forests of stone surrounding him. Spires many times taller than the tallest tree he had ever seen seemed to press down on him, surround him. His heart raced. The young coyote cowered and trembled from the inescapable truth. "I am so lost," he whimpered.

10

A Bird's-Eye View

Mischief kept an eye on the coyote as he explored the city. The crow had hoped to see more entertaining encounters between the coyote and the humans, but so far things had been pretty dull.

Mischief followed overhead. Humans peddled past on bicycles, rode by in taxicabs, even ran along on their two legs, and never once did they notice the coyote loping along the sidewalk. It never ceased to amaze the crow how little humans saw.

"Time to stir things up," the crow chortled.

He swooped down and pecked the coyote on the head.

"Ow!" Trouble yipped. He swerved and raced down the sidewalk.

"Hee!" Mischief crowed. He dived down again and plucked a bill full of fur from Trouble's tail.

Trouble tucked his tail between his legs and looked for someplace, any place, to get away from this menace in the sky.

Whoosh! To Trouble's utter astonishment, an opening appeared in the smooth stone wall he'd been running beside.

Before the crow had a chance to peck him again, the coyote veered through the doorway and into the biggest den he had ever seen. His feet skidded and slipped on a floor as smooth and shiny as water.

"Can I help—" a voice said, then "Eeeeeek!"

Trouble froze at the sound of the screaming Maker. He pressed his belly against the cold floor and waited for whatever would happen next.

Whoosh!

The security guard, who always claimed nothing interesting ever happened in a life insurance building, strolled through the automatic doors, bearing a tray of coffee.

Caw! Caw!

Mischief flew past the guard and made straight for Trouble.

The receptionist, Molly Valentine, who secretly wrote TV scripts at work precisely because nothing interesting ever happened in a life insurance building,

41

screamed at the sight of the coyote and crow.

"Help!" she cried. "Help!"

The guard dropped the tray of hot coffee.

Mischief dive-bombed the coyote.

Trouble scrambled to his feet and skittered across the shiny floor, barely keeping his paws beneath him, desperately looking for any escape from the horrid bird and the screaming Maker.

"Stop!" ordered the guard. "Stop this instant!"

Ding!

Mischief flew around to the side of the confused coyote and gave him a good peck on the ear.

"Yow!" Trouble bolted away from the crow and right into the waiting elevator.

With Mischief's final, gleeful peck at the bright red button, the elevator doors closed.

11

Officer Vetch

The calls started coming in to New York City Animal Control and Welfare early that morning.

The first call came from a produce truck driver over on 154th Street claiming a coyote had stowed away in her truck.

"Highly unlikely," Officer Vetch snorted.

The owner of a diner three blocks east of 154th Street called next. He said a coyote had raided his garbage cans. "And made a right mess of things too," he added.

"Doubtful," Officer Vetch proclaimed.

And then, at 10:03, came the call from Long Life Security Insurance by the security guard, one Timothy

Buckle. "There's a coyote in our elevator!"

"Hmmm . . . ," Officer Vetch mused. "Lock down the building," he barked into the phone. "I'll be there in ten minutes."

Some people might think a coyote in an elevator was the most improbable, preposterous, outrageous report an animal control officer could receive. But to Officer Vetch, this seemed like just the kind of thing a coyote in the city would do.

Trouble turned one way and then another in the small, shining den. His reflection rippled like it had in a pool at the bottom of Singing Creek. He glanced up. There was no sky, no canopy of leaves or clouds. Then again, there wasn't that annoying bird either, or the sound of the screeching female Maker.

Trouble investigated the peculiar space. Overlapping scents of Makers—salty smells, sweet smells, the scent of anxiety, the scent of excitement, the scent of boredom—filled the tiny den.

And there, just there, the aroma of food. He was so, so hungry! He licked the bagel crumbs from the carpeted floor. Licking the carpet made him thirsty. Food and water were what he needed.

He looked for the door through which he'd come. It was gone. He searched the corners for it, but they were as solid as stone. He pawed at what he thought had been the entrance to the den, but it was solid too. Trouble dug frantically at the carpeted floor. Once he'd found himself shut inside the Maker's shed back at the farm when he'd been investigating a sack of chicken feed. Digging out under the door to the shed had taken some time and effort, but he'd been home for dinner.

This time, though, no matter how hard he dug, he could not get out. He was trapped.

Trouble huddled in the corner of the elevator and panted with anxiety.

As promised, Officer Vetch arrived outside the Long Life Security Insurance building ten minutes later. He double-parked his truck and left blue and red lights flashing.

Mischief watched from the chandelier high above as the man strode purposefully into the lobby.

"Officer Ambrose Vetch," he said to the security guard, "from New York City Animal Control and Welfare."

Mischief narrowed his eyes. He committed the name and face of this particular human to memory.

"Is the alleged coyote still in the elevator?" Officer Vetch asked, clutching the catch pole.

The security guard motioned him over to the reception desk. "Come see for yourself," he said. "We have a security camera in the elevator."

The guard poked at the keyboard with one finger. Slowly, the camera inside the elevator panned to the left.

Officer Vetch held his breath.

"There," the guard said, jabbing at the screen.

Sure enough, huddled in the corner, eyes glazed with terror, big ears pinned flat against its head, long pointy snout twitching was, without a doubt, a coyote.

"Here's the plan, Buckle," Officer Vetch said. "We'll lock the front doors.

"Then," Vetch continued, "when I give you the signal, unlock the elevator. I'll open the doors, and, before the coyote knows what it's about, I'll get him in my noose."

Molly Valentine frowned. "You're not going to kill it, are you?" She eyed the gun in his holster.

Vetch strode over to the elevator. "Oh no," he called across the lobby. "The zoo will be very happy to add him to their collection."

Trouble, who had gone into a panic-induced trance, jumped at the sound of a Maker's voice. He shot straight up in the air, bouncing from one side of the elevator to the other.

Ding!

The elevator lurched beneath Trouble's feet. He felt the den rising and rising.

Officer Vetch watched in disbelief as the elevator rose up to the first floor, then the second, then the third, then the fourth.

"What's happened?" he roared.

He dropped his pole and raced over to the desk where Timothy Buckle and Molly Valentine stared at the monitor with wide eyes.

"He, he must have accidentally pushed the buttons inside the elevator," Molly Valentine stammered.

"Well, do something," Vetch commanded. "Bring him down."

The crow had already beaten him to it.

As soon as Mischief saw Officer Vetch drop the catch pole, he knew this was his chance.

While the humans stared at the monitor, the crow flew down from the chandelier. Using his sharp black bill, he pecked at the elevator's Down button.

Ding! Ding!

Officer Vetch, Timothy Buckle, and Molly Valentine turned toward the sound.

The elevator door slid open.

The terrified (and somewhat nauseated) coyote took one wobbly step out.

The security guard whimpered.

Molly Valentine's mouth formed a small O.

Vetch eyed the distance between himself and the catch pole.

"Run!" the crow screamed.

Just for the briefest moment, Trouble and Officer Vetch locked eyes. In the coyote's eyes, the Maker saw the unknowable wild; in the Maker's eyes, the coyote saw the hunter, locked on his prey. Trouble had seen those same eyes when he had been hunted from above by the eagle. But this time, his father was not here to save him.

Trouble bolted from the elevator; Officer Vetch lunged for his catch pole.

Let it be noted that a tray full of coffee spilled on a marble floor creates a very slippery situation.

Vetch's feet flew out from under him. He landed on his back with a loud "Oof!"

Timothy Buckle, who before this morning had been quite convinced nothing interesting ever happened in a life insurance building, attempted to pull his nightstick from his holster as Trouble careened by.

Molly Valentine screamed.

Mischief dive-bombed the security guard.

The last thing Officer Vetch saw as he pulled himself to his feet was a great, bushy tail with a black tip streaming out the front doors and, curiously, a crow right behind.

12

What's in a Name

Trouble ran as fast as he had ever run, away from the horror of the elevator and the Long Life Security Insurance building.

A siren wailed in the distance. A sudden, fierce longing for his family washed over the young coyote.

"I want to go home," he whimpered.

The hot pavement burned Trouble's pads. He felt thirstier than he could ever remember feeling. He loped along, his long tongue lolling out the side of his mouth. Oh, what he wouldn't give to plunge his whole body into the shaded pools at the bottom of Singing Creek. What he wouldn't give for the cool, soft grass of the meadow.

And then, as if an especially curious, overly trouble-some coyote's wishes had come true, Trouble smelled water. He followed his long, pointy nose down one street, up an avenue, and across a courtyard.

There he saw it, shining and splashing in all its glory: a waterfall! An odd waterfall, in an upside-down kind of way, but that didn't matter to Trouble. It was wet and it was cool.

Pressing his body into the shadows, Trouble crept toward the fountain. Mischief landed on a utility pole. He looked up the street one way and down the other.

"Okay," he called. "The coast is clear."

Trouble was so hot and so thirsty, he didn't stop to wonder if the crow was pulling yet another one of his pranks. Instead, he leaped into the fountain. He splashed and yipped and let the falling water spill into his open mouth.

He could have stayed in that cool water all day.

Mischief glided down from the utility pole and landed silently on the edge of the fountain. With a gleam in his eye, he scooped up a bill full of water and splashed Trouble right in the face.

"Hey!" the coyote yipped. "I was relaxing!"

"Not anymore," Mischief chortled, and churned the water with his wings.

"Ha," Trouble yipped. "Two can play this game."

He used his long snout like a shovel and flung water on the bird.

Mischief cawed with delight. He plopped into the fountain and flailed the coyote with water and wings. Trouble slapped the water with his front paws like Twist had taught him, creating a tsunami in the small fountain.

Someone laughed.

Coyote and crow froze.

A female Maker stood just feet from the fountain, grinning.

Suddenly, Trouble noticed many, many Makers streaming from the tall, shiny caves surrounding the fountain. Most trotted surprisingly fast on their two legs, holding something to their ears; others walked with heads down, looking intently at a small something held in their hands. None of these Makers saw the crow and the coyote in the fountain.

Except this one.

She laughed again. "A dog and a bird playing together in the fountain. How adorable."

She set her lunch bag on the ground and fished around in her purse. "I just have to get a picture of you two," she said.

Trouble slunk from the fountain and scurried behind a thick screen of bamboo.

Mischief, never one to miss an opportunity for a free meal *and* a chance to be annoying, launched himself from the fountain straight to the woman's lunch bag and snatched it up.

"Hey!" the woman cried. "That's my lunch!"

"Was," Mischief cawed from the top of the pole. He lifted up in the air, bag swinging from his bill, and flew off.

He swooped low over the coyote and cruised around the back of the building. Trouble followed the delicious scent of food.

By the time Trouble found him, the crow had ripped the bag apart and was cataloging its contents: ham and cheese sandwich, carrot sticks, potato chips, and blueberry muffin. "Not bad," Mischief said.

He heard a groan. He looked up from his bounty into the hungry eyes of Trouble.

"I am so, so hungry," Trouble whimpered.

Mischief had not shared a single, solitary thing since he'd left the nest. As far as he was concerned, in the city it was every critter for himself.

But something pricked the crow's mind; something even deeper stirred his black crow heart.

"Oh, what the heck," he said.

He flung the baggie containing the sandwich to the ground and, in an astonishing display of selflessness, the muffin too.

Trouble pounced on the sandwich and muffin and gulped them down, plastic baggies and all.

"Oh, kid," the crow said, "you're going to regret that later."

But Trouble didn't hear the crow. The food had taken the edge off the gnawing hunger in his belly. Now, what he wanted more than anything else was to take a nap.

He curled up in a cool, dark corner on a side street.

The crow fluttered down to the pavement and walked over to the coyote.

"What's your name?" Mischief asked.

Trouble regarded the crow. Finally, he said, "My parents call me Trouble."

Mischief couldn't help himself. He chirped. He chortled. Then he cackled. "Trouble? Your parents named you *Trouble*? Perfect!" he crowed.

Trouble had half a mind to bite the annoying bird, but he was too tired. Instead, he asked, "Well, what's your name?"

"My mother called me Gregor the Mischief Maker," the crow said, "but everyone just calls me Mischief."

"Ha!" Trouble barked. "Talk about the perfect name, you're nothing but mischief."

"Yeah," Mischief said, with just a tinge of longing, "that's what my mother said."

The image of his own mother filled Trouble's mind

and his heart. Oh, she must be so worried about him!

"Just a little rest," he mumbled. "Just a little rest and then I'll find my way back to the Beast. I'll even be home in time for supper."

And with that the coyote tucked his nose under his tail, closed his eyes, and slept.

13

Amelia and Rosebud

It's not true the City never sleeps.

In the small, quiet hours of the night, bankers slept. Bartenders slept. Café workers slept, and dog walkers slept. Even delivery truck drivers slept.

A poet and her dog slept, dancers slept, mothers and fathers and their children slept.

That is, all except one child, a most curious girl named Amelia.

The girl was curious about many things, but particularly animals, particularly those Furred and Feathered who lived among the humans in the city.

Amelia lifted her binoculars to her eyes and peered out her bedroom window. The week before, on a moonless night, she had seen what she hoped was an opossum drinking from a puddle on the sidewalk. She very much wanted to add North America's only marsupial to her list of city sightings.

The girl had, in fact, seen an opossum that night. An opossum named Rosebud.

As opossums go, she was a pretty little thing.

Rosebud had black-button eyes, a nose the most delicate shade of pink, front paws shaped like small stars, and fur as soft as a whisper.

As the city grew dark, Rosebud woke from her long nap. The days had been so beastly hot that she had taken to sleeping in one of the city's grander subway stations. The tile floor, although hard, was cool. She had found the perfect sleeping nook in an air vent missing its cover. There, it was dark and cool and away from the hundreds of humans coming and going. And even better, some of her favorite things to eat—spiders, cockroaches, even the occasional beetle—could be had without ever leaving the safety of the station.

It had been over a week since the little opossum had been outside. Although Rosebud was a wild creature, she was utterly terrified of the Outside.

Opossums are by nature timid and gentle. Faced with a threat, they may hiss and snarl and spit, but they'd rather play dead than fight.

Even among the Opossum Clan, though, Rosebud was singular in her lack of bravery.

But opossums do not, cannot, live by bugs alone. As reluctant as she was to venture out from the safety of her home, a gnawing hunger drove her more.

Rosebud peeked out of the air vent. She sniffed the air for humans.

She listened for the sound of footsteps.

She did not hear the constant rise and fall of the humans' voices, nor the click and shuffle of their feet.

She did not hear the rattle and hum of the subway trains.

Warily, Rosebud scuttled across the gleaming floor and tiptoed up the wide stairs. There, just across another expanse of stone, stood the doors to the Outside. She looked one way and then the other. A human in a uniform sat in a tipped-back chair, arms folded over his belly, eyes closed, mouth hanging open.

Rosebud did her opossum best to gather all the courage she could find. Her whiskers trembled with fright.

"You can do it," she said to herself in her mother's voice. "Just take it one step at a time."

Rosebud placed one paw in front of the other—one step, then another, and another—until she stood staring up at the huge glass doors, and then *whoosh!* The doors slid open and Rosebud stepped into the great Outside.

14

Coyote Dreams

Trouble's feet twitched and jerked in his sleep as he raced Pounce and Swift across the wide, green meadows. His tail thumped once in joy at the sight of his mother and father and his big brother, Twist. There they stood, grinning their wide coyote grins, in their beautiful forest, and everywhere, everywhere, the sky. "Oh, how I've missed you," he whimpered.

Then he heard it, the most beautiful sound in the world: all of them singing together the Song to the Moon.

Something wet woke the coyote. One raindrop, then another. He opened his eyes, expecting to see his family, his home.

Instead, he saw the stone forest and canyons and the hard, bare ground. And that was not the full moon shining down, casting shadows. It was a streetlight, throwing shadows in the dark.

Dark!

Panic swept over the pup. He had slept too long! The Maker and the Beast would have returned to their farm by now. How would he find his way home?

The coyote paced back and forth, looking anxiously at the sky. The buildings were so tall and towering, he could not tell where the tops ended and the night sky began. Storm clouds obscured the moon. The North Star was nowhere in sight.

Trouble threw back his head and pointed his muzzle to the moonless, starless sky. He took a deep breath and sang his despair. *Where are you?* he sang. *Where is my home?*

Rats and cats hunting and being hunted cowered at the sound of the coyote. Trouble's yips disturbed the dreams of a poet. They woke the poet's dog. The girl, Amelia, slipped from her bed, raised her bedroom window, and looked out into the night through her binoculars.

Trouble's howls froze Rosebud in her tracks.

Trouble's yaps woke Mischief.

"What's your problem?" he grumbled.

"Where is the Beast that brought me to this place?" Trouble asked. "I have to get back there!"

"You mean the produce truck?"

"Yes, the Beast," he barked. "I have to get back to it so I can go home."

Mischief fluffed his feathers against the drizzle now falling from the sky. He sighed. "It's just a truck, not some beast, and that truck's long gone."

"My big brother, Twist, always told me to find the North Star in the night sky if I ever got lost, and it would guide me home," Trouble said. He looked at the buildings surrounding him, pressing in on him, blocking the sky. "How will I ever see it? How will I ever find my way home?" he wailed in that way only a heartbroken coyote can.

The rain came down in earnest. Thunder rumbled, and lightning lit the sky.

Trouble cowered and trembled.

Normally, Trouble was not afraid of a little rain. He actually enjoyed it. But the Singing Creek pups had been born in early spring, in the time of gentle rain and no thunder or lightning. That is, until this night.

Boom! Crack! Thunder shook the ground and echoed through the canyon of skyscrapers. Lightning turned the sky silver.

With a yip, Trouble dashed into the street looking for a place to escape.

"Wait!" Mischief called.

Trouble skittered around one corner and then another, knocking over trash cans, scattering the rats, until he came face-to-face, almost whisker-to-whisker, with an opossum named Rosebud.

"Oh!" said Trouble.

Eeek! squeaked Rosebud.

Caw! said Mischief.

"Whoa," said Amelia, peering through her binoculars.

Rosebud whirled and raced as fast as an opossum can (which is not terribly fast, as four-footed animals go), back the way she came.

Whoosh went the doors to the train station.

Rosebud skittered across the lobby, past the sleeping night watchman, and down the wide stairs, Trouble following close behind.

Whoosh! Mischief flew into the subway station on Trouble's heels.

The opossum raced across the marble floor, heart pounding. *This is it,* she thought. *I will be eaten, and no one will mourn my passing because I am all alone in the world.*

If only she could stand her ground like the raccoons

she had seen who took on dogs twice their size, maybe she could save herself from the coyote. But she was not brave like a raccoon; she was not even brave like most opossums.

Instead, she headed straight for the open door of a waiting subway train idling on the tracks.

Rosebud scuttled inside the empty train car and curled beneath the last seat in the back. She closed her eyes tight and prayed to the patron saint of opossums that the coyote would not find her.

Trouble stopped midway across the grand station. He gazed in disbelief at the soaring, shining room, his fear forgotten. Never had he seen anything so astonishing. It could only be the work of the Makers, and it was a wondrous thing. True, there was no grass beneath his feet and not a single tree in sight, but it shimmered and shone in a golden light as if it held the moon.

Caw! Caw!

The night watchman awoke with a start. "Hey, what're you doing in here, you stupid bird?" the watchman bellowed. "And wait, is that a coyote?"

"Here we go again," Mischief muttered.

The crow swooped down and snatched the pointed tip of Trouble's enormous ear. "Move!" he called.

Trouble yipped. He bolted straight through the

open doors of the subway car, Mischief right on the coyote's tail.

Whoosh! The doors closed, the train lurched.

And so it was that an opossum named Rosebud, a crow named Mischief, and a young coyote named Trouble raced away in a subway car into the dawn.

15

Trouble on a Train

Trouble was trapped. He knew it as surely as when the doors to the produce truck slammed shut, as surely as when the doors to the elevator closed. He knew as sure as he knew his own name that he was in trouble once again.

He jumped up onto the hard seat and looked out the window at the lights ticking by.

"What now?" he asked, glaring at the crow.

Mischief's claws grasped the back of a seat as he pecked at a piece of dried chewing gum. "Not much to do until the train comes to the next stop," Mischief replied, prying loose the piece of pink gum. "Just relax and enjoy the ride."

A thousand questions ran through the pup's mind: What was a train? Was it yet another type of Beast? And what would happen when this thing stopped? Would he be closer to his home and his family? It was all just too much to think about.

The gentle rocking of the train and the steady *clack click clack* put Trouble in a trance. Slowly, oh so slowly, his eyes closed, his head drooped, and he fell fast asleep.

Rosebud clutched her long, hairless tail to her chest and listened. She'd heard the crow and the coyote talking at the front of the train car. Now all was quiet.

It was not the first time the opossum had ridden in a subway train. Twice before in winter months she had scuttled into a subway car late at night looking for a warm place out of the wind and snow. She never failed to find a tasty treat or two underneath the seats. As her mother had said, "Humans are purely gifted when it comes to making trash." It was her mother's opinion that an opossum would fare best in the wide world by living close to humans.

Rosebud wasn't so sure. She found most everything associated with the world of humans—their cars, their dogs, their bright lights, the things they threw at her—frightening. But worst of all, on seeing Rosebud, they said the rudest and most hurtful things. They would shriek; they would cry out in alarm. They called her "ugly," "icky," "pointy," "filthy," and the worst— oh, the worst!—"rodent." No insult cut deeper than being compared to a dirty, smelly, untrustworthy, conniving rat.

Rosebud was a very sensitive soul.

Trouble slept past the first stop, the second stop, and the third stop.

Mischief watched the bright lights tick past and wondered what to do. Every time the doors slid open, he prepared to fly away from this space, a space too small for a winged creature. He longed to stretch his wings and soar into the dawn sky. But yet, and yet . . . there was a coyote and an opossum in a subway car, and the city was waking. The possibilities were endless.

The train eased to a stop. The doors slid open. Voices woke the coyote.

"Look at that cute puppy!"

"What's a bird doing in a subway car?"

"Unattended animals are not allowed on trains," a tall gentleman proclaimed, waving an umbrella. The umbrella, having a mind of its own, snapped open with a pop.

Trouble yipped in panic. He leaped off the bench,

bolted toward the door, only to be blocked by the open umbrella. He dashed to the front, bounced from one side of the car to the other, then raced for the back, cowering close to Rosebud.

"It's mad!" someone cried.

"Call the police!"

"Stand aside," an authoritative voice commanded.

A woman in an official uniform pushed through the spectators waiting to board the train. She removed an impressive flashlight from her wide belt, clicked on the light, and shined it into the subway car. Into the black eyes of Mischief and, in the back, the yellow eyes of Trouble.

She slipped a radio from her belt (a belt that held many shiny things, Mischief noted) and barked into it, "Dispatch, I got a situation here. There's some kind of trouble on the train."

The MTA worker, Verla Trumpowski, straightened her hat and waved aside the bystanders. "I'm going in to take a look-see," she said.

She drew her nightstick and stepped into the train. "Don't you try any funny business," she said, pointing her stick at the crow and coyote.

The light from her flashlight swept from one end of the subway car to the other.

Trouble tried to make himself as small as possible;

Mischief greedily eyed the shiny objects dangling from Verla Trumpowski's belt.

Rosebud chose this moment to put some distance between herself and the coyote. She crept out from under the seat; she froze at the sight of the tall thing in front of her.

Verla Trumpowski caught a movement from the corner of her eye. She shined her beam on something pointy and white. It must be said that neither Rosebud nor Verla Trumpowski had very good eyesight.

The human froze.

Rosebud realized through her keen sense of smell that this was a human. Her heart pounded. Her blood froze. She could feel a faint coming on.

Although Rosebud was not the bravest of creatures, she was practical. She decided the best course of action was to assure this human that 1) she was not a threat, and 2) she was not a rat.

Rosebud stood up on her hind legs, pulled back her lips in an enormous smile, revealing all fifty of her gloriously sharp teeth.

Without a sound, Verla Trumpowski fainted onto the floor.

Mischief croaked in disbelief. "How did that beady-eyed little thing do that?"

The coyote didn't know and didn't care. All he

knew was that the odd creature had just saved him from certain disaster.

Trouble leaped down from the bench, gave Rosebud a huge, sloppy lick of thanks and relief. "Oh, *thank you*! Thank you, friend!"

But Rosebud did not hear Trouble's effusive words of thanks; the sight of the coyote's open mouth coming right at her (not to mention her close encounter with the human) was all too much for the opossum. She fainted dead away.

"Look!" someone cried from the growing crowd on the subway platform. "That dog attacked that woman!"

"Get it!"

"Help her!

"Call the police!"

Uh-oh. Trouble had heard those words before. He needed to get out of there, fast.

Trouble glanced at the angry crowd outside the open door of subway train, then down at the little opossum.

"I can't leave her," he said. "She saved me."

While it was true that Trouble was not one for rules, the one rule of the Coyote Clan he took to heart was this: you never, ever left a member of the pack behind. This strange little creature had saved his life. As far as Trouble was concerned, that made her a member of his pack.

There was only one thing, and one thing only, to do: carefully, Trouble grabbed the opossum by the scruff of her neck, just the way his mother had done when he was a pup, and trotted out of the train and onto the platform.

The crowd gasped and parted as the coyote, head held high, opossum dangling from his jaws, trotted quickly toward the stairs and the waking city above.

16

The Wild in the City

The coyote's jaws ached. Although Rosebud was just a wee opossum, smaller than your average opossum, she was heavier than the sticks and bones Trouble had carried in play with his brother and sisters.

Oh so carefully, he set Rosebud on the ground and sniffed her from the tip of her pink, pointy snout to the end of her hairless tail. She smelled of banana peels, popcorn, and most strongly, the sour smell of fear.

Trouble nudged her with his nose. He heard her heart quicken.

The sun climbed the sides of the tall buildings; car horns honked and traffic rumbled. The city was awakening. Trouble needed to find a place to hide, but he could not leave this odd little creature behind.

Mischief landed on a tree branch above the coyote. He jangled the keys stolen from Verla Trumpowski's belt, delighting in their sound.

"What do I do now?" Trouble asked. "There's nowhere to hide, and"—he nudged Rosebud again—"she acts like she's dead."

"That's what an opossum does best," Mischief said.

Trouble regarded the stiff legs pointing skyward, the tongue hanging between white, pointy teeth, the closed eyes. "She's doing a pretty good job," he said with admiration. "But I can't leave her here. She could get hurt."

Mischief sighed. He really didn't understand why the coyote bothered with the rat-like thing. Oh sure, he knew opossums and rats had no more in common than a crow and the pigeons infesting Central Park. But who cared about an opossum?

"I know a place we can go," Mischief said. "It's not close, though."

Trouble looked at the little marsupial lying prostrate on the ground. What would Twist do?

Once again, Trouble picked up Rosebud by the scruff of her neck.

Mischief pushed off from the tree branch, still

holding Verla Trumpowski's keys in his bill. He flew low over the coyote and opossum, leading the way.

That way led through a confusing warren of dark side streets and across a wide, busy street. Twice Trouble had to stop, drop Rosebud, rest his jaws, then pick her up again. Really, he thought, a rabbit would be much easier. Or a mouse.

Finally, just when Trouble didn't think he could carry the opossum any farther, they broke free of yet another dark, damp side street and out into the sun. The sun!

Trouble gasped and dropped Rosebud in astonishment. There before him, as far as the eye could see, were trees! And not only trees, there was grass and bushes and flowers and the smell of water.

And oh, the birds! Birds everywhere, singing and chirping and squabbling. Trouble never thought he would be so utterly happy to hear birds.

Rosebud felt something cool and soft beneath her. She smelled flowers and bugs and the heady scent of rich dirt, all things she hadn't smelled since she was a baby. It was so wonderful, she forgot to be afraid. She opened her eyes. She was greeted by the sight of wide blue sky and the green tops of trees.

"It's beautiful," she sighed.

"It's the wild," Trouble said in a reverent whisper.

"We're not out of the woods yet," Mischief called.

"I'm willing to bet that Vetch is still looking for you."

Trouble cocked his head to one side. "What's a Vetch?"

"Not a what but a who," Mischief said. "He's that human who tried to catch you yesterday."

Trouble looked behind him. There, just feet away, cars and trucks and Makers hurried by. An odor, faint but menacing in its familiarity, hung in the air. A smell that evoked the eyes of the hunter: Officer Vetch.

He looked down at Rosebud. "The crow's right. We have to go farther, and quickly."

The end of the opossum's nose blushed red with embarrassment. "I don't think I can keep up with you."

Trouble looked at the city, the forest, and back at the opossum. Then he lay down on the grass. "Can you climb on?" he asked.

Of course she could. Hadn't she and her brothers and sisters spent months riding on their mama's back?

In seconds she sprawled across the coyote's back, paws clutching the ruff around his neck.

They crossed a wide paved trail lined with benches, then slipped through a hedgerow and down a hill to the biggest meadow Trouble had ever seen. The sight of trees, the wide sweep of grass made Trouble's heart ache for his family.

Still, this huge meadow provided no place to hide. "Is there a forest?" he asked the crow.

"This way," the crow answered.

They climbed a low hill, crossed one bridge and then another. To Trouble's delight, he heard the soft music of a meandering stream. Trouble wanted so very much to investigate the rocks, but his coyote instinct urged him to find cover.

He trotted farther into the deep green of the forest. They skirted a small, jewel-like pond surrounded by azalea bushes. Beautiful, but still not what Trouble sought.

And then, just around the corner, there it was: an ancient, crumbling stone wall covered by decades of intertwining strands of ivy, honeysuckle, and blackberry canes.

Trouble slipped into a surprisingly large den hidden behind a screen of rock and bushes. He could easily have slept with his brother and sisters in this hideaway.

He circled once, circled twice, then curled up tight with his nose buried under the tip of his tail. He didn't feel the little opossum curl up against him; he didn't see Mischief hide the keys in the hollow of a tree, nor did he smell the squirrel who poked his head into the den to investigate. For the first time in two days, Trouble felt safe and he slept.

The pup slept even as the sun reached the top of

the sky and people filled the park. He slept as lovers picnicked in the meadow, as children sailed small boats across the pond, as runners checked their heart rates.

Trouble did not hear the excited yips of the dogs and people playing fetch in the meadow; he did not hear the *clip clop* of horses pulling carriages, the cluck and coo of pigeons, the constant chatter of squirrels.

He even slept through a late-afternoon thunderstorm.

Finally, at dusk, thirst and hunger woke him. Careful not to disturb the sleeping opossum, Trouble crept from his den. He stretched his long legs, first one back leg and then the other, and sniffed the air. Downhill from his den, he smelled water and heard a rustle.

He saw a squirrel scurry from the rocks bordering a small cove on the lake.

His stomach rumbled.

He crept behind a long curtain of willow branches, staying downwind of the squirrel.

When he was just a few feet from the unsuspecting creature, he gathered his hind legs beneath him and arced up in the air and down onto his dinner. His brother, Pounce, would have been proud.

17

Wildborn

Trouble licked the last of the squirrel from his paws, then took a long drink. For the first time in two days, he felt rested and satiated. His curiosity returned by leaps and bounds.

He climbed to the top of a large boulder and gazed across the lake. Never had he seen so much water, stretching as far as his eyes could see. He could hear and smell Makers coming and going along the paved trail he had crossed earlier. The wildness in him trembled at the thought of encountering more of them.

But then there was the trouble part of him.

Keeping to the shadows, he slunk back up the hill. He crept as close as he dared to this place thick with the scent of Makers and settled under a wild tangle of forsythia.

Never in his short life had Trouble ever imagined so many Makers—young Makers, old Makers, Makers running (although Trouble never could see what chased them, or what, for that matter, they were chasing), Makers riding atop skeletons of small Beasts, and even Makers with wheels on their feet. It was all so fascinating!

And then Trouble saw the most curious sight of all: dogs leading Makers by long strings! Trouble knew what dogs were from his visits to the Maker's home on the edge of the forest. He knew they always lived with Makers, which seemed an odd thing to do.

He heard a flutter and a rustle. Mischief hopped over to the coyote.

"Why do the dogs lead them?" Trouble watched a tall, thin Maker pulled along by a dog no bigger than a rabbit. "Are the Makers blind? Are they too dumb to find their way?" It had not escaped the coyote's notice how very small the Makers' noses and ears were.

Mischief chortled. "You got that right. Humans, which is what they're called, are not the brightest, if you get my meaning."

Trouble wasn't entirely sure he did. But before

he could ask Mischief what he meant, he saw something he could never have imagined: A Maker—a human—carefully used a plastic bag to pick up the waste its leader dog had deposited in the grass and—oh!—carried it along with her.

Trouble looked at Mischief in disbelief. "The Makers—er, humans—*worship* the dogs?" It was the only possible explanation, wasn't it?

Mischief cawed with delight.

The sky grew dark. The parade of humans along the paved trail waned, then stopped altogether.

For the first time, away from the towering buildings and streetlights, Trouble saw stars in a wide blanket of purple sky. Still, the light from the city washed the North Star from the sky.

"Soon," he said to Rosebud as she washed her face and whiskers, "the moon will be out."

Rosebud paused. "I do not like the moon," she said. "Especially the full moon."

Trouble blinked. "How can you not like the moon? The moon is the mother. My father says the moon is Divine Light."

"Exactly," Rosebud said. "Let's see how much you like that 'Divine Light' if you're being hunted to eat." Her whiskers quivered.

Trouble considered this. He had rarely been hunted for food, but he did know a lot about the moon.

"I think," he said carefully, "that sometimes you have to take risks to see something beautiful."

Finally, the moon rose. Trouble watched it slowly climb, not above the jagged tops of trees like at home, but above the jagged New York City skyline in the distance.

Rosebud peered out from their den in the bramble and looked west. A half moon rested on its side in the sky. She sighed with relief. She ambled out and stood next to Trouble.

"Do you think," the coyote mused, "this is the same moon that rises over our meadow by Singing Creek? The moon we sing to?"

Rosebud looked from the moon to the coyote. "I don't know," she said. "I've never thought about that. I've lived most of my life in the city, under this sky."

The two friends watched the moon together, one with a longing in his heart and the other with more questions than she had ever known.

"Perhaps," she said, "we should ask the crow. Birds go many places opossums don't."

Frogs began their evening song; fireflies floated from the forest on the far side of the meadow, blinking. A bat careened through the sky.

Trouble stood and shook off his pondering. It was time to explore.

"Come on," he said to Rosebud.

They scouted the edge of the inlet. Rosebud discovered for the first time the particular deliciousness of fresh frog. Trouble discovered catching one was much harder than it looked, although the fun was in the trying.

They investigated the wide meadow where grass held the smells of Makers, dogs, and food. The two friends shared the remains of a peanut butter and jelly sandwich. Rosebud's ears trembled with delight at the sight of a coyote with peanut butter stuck to the roof of his mouth.

They crossed another of the humans' paved trails and came, finally, to a lovely forest glen.

Crickets chorused and the moon stood high in the sky, and just for a moment Trouble was home with his family.

He threw back his head, closed his eyes, and sang,

Oh Mother Moon, rising in the sky,
we welcome you back on this summer night.
We will hunt by your light.
We will love by your light.
We will dance by your light.

Oh Mother Moon, rising in the sky,
we welcome you,
we sing to you,
Mother Moon in the sky.

The forest grew quiet. Rosebud gazed up at the coyote in astonishment. Mischief alighted on a branch close by.

Trouble listened for the answering voices of his pack. None came. He knew, then, they must be very far away.

Heartbroken, he sang his longing to the moon.

Where is my home in the forest
on this moonlit night?
With my mother and father and family.
They are my heart. They are my home.
Where is my home?
Where is my home
on this moonlit night?

The last high note of Trouble's song sailed through the night.

"Oh my, oh my," said a voice. "That was quite something."

Trouble opened his eyes. In the glen sat a fox, her

red-and-white coat shimmering in the moonlight. Rosebud gasped and hid between Trouble's legs.

"The last note was a bit sharp," a sonorous voice said from the top of an old cherry tree, "and the rhyming scheme lacked acceptable meter."

Trouble peered up into the trees. There, standing tall on a limb, huge eyes shining as bright as twin moons, perched a great horned owl. It glared down at the coyote with disdain.

"It's better than anything you could do," Mischief snapped.

The owl drew himself up, teetering just a bit on the branch. "Uncouth cad," he hissed.

The fox flicked the white tip of her tail. "That song made me think of the den where I was born. Such happy times, they were. I'm raising my own kits in that very same den where my mother raised me. Home is family, isn't it?"

"Home is everywhere," Mischief declared. "Home is all that I see."

Rosebud thought about home too. Home had once been deep in her mother's pouch, then riding on her mother's back. But her family had long ago gone its separate ways.

Trouble looked back up at the sky. He heard crickets, yes, and the wind in the trees. But farther beyond, yet not so far, he heard pulsing traffic, bleating horns, wailing sirens, and the restless world of Makers.

"This is not my home," he said.

"Then might I suggest," the owl said with a menacing click of his talons, "you go back from whence you came?"

"But I don't know how to get back to my home," Trouble said.

"Just skulk away like the good little scavenger you are," the owl said, "and retrace your steps back to wherever you came from."

All eyes turned to Trouble.

"But it's not that easy," he said.

And then, as the moon traced its way across the summer sky, past the Milky Way and the Big Dipper, Trouble told his story. He told them about the Singing Creek Pack, and the wide green meadow, and the den beneath the roots of an old oak tree, and the sky that went on forever.

He told them about wanting to see what was beyond his home and the Maker's house, and his plan, and the long ride in the belly of the Beast, and all that had happened since, including the terrible Officer Vetch and the big woman in the subway train and all the Makers screaming and yelling and threatening.

They listened without a sound beneath the moon.

"That's it," Trouble said. "That's how I got here."

"You are Wildborn," the fox whispered.

The others nodded, including the owl.

"Wildborn," they said with reverence.

18

Minette

The next morning, the poet and the poodle did what they did every morning: they rose from their beds in the gray light of dawn. They ate their poached eggs and toast; brushed teeth, hair, and fur; and went out to see what the morning would bring.

Minette, the poodle, yawned. She had not slept well because of the howling that had awakened her the night before.

It was not unusual to hear dogs howling in the city, especially in the summer when apartment windows were open to let in the cool night air. But this howling was different in ways Minette could not name but felt in her bones.

Minette and the poet, Madame Reveuse, locked their apartment door and rode the elevator down eight floors. Minette's toenails clicked on the worn marble floor of the lobby as she trotted beside Madame.

"*Bonjour*," Madame Reveuse said to the doorman.

"And good morning to you," the doorman said as he pulled open the door. As always, he patted the top of Minette's fine, curly head, something she did not particularly like but tolerated nonetheless. It would have been rude to do otherwise.

The sky was just turning from pale gray to pink, the streets almost deserted. A newspaper deliveryman removed bundles of papers from the trunk of his car. A shopkeeper swept the sidewalk in front of her bakery. A doorman stood outside a grand apartment building smoking a cigarette.

Madame Reveuse and Minette strode down West Seventy-Second Street. At 6:30 in the morning, they had Manhattan mostly and blissfully to themselves.

Until they arrived at the west entrance to Central Park. There, they joined the small but dedicated pack of early-morning dogs and their walkers.

Madame unclipped the leash from Minette's sparkling pink collar. "Go play," she said, though they both knew she wouldn't. Minette was not a game player or ball chaser. She most certainly was not one to roll in anything, smelly or otherwise. What was the point of getting her lovely coat dirty?

The poet and the poodle followed the winding paths past Strawberry Fields, Cherry Hill, over Bow Bridge (Minette's personal favorite of all the Central Park bridges), and into the deep green of The Ramble. There, the poet sat on a bench perched on a dome of ancient stone and removed a pad of paper and a pen. It was here she composed the poems for which she was famous.

Once she was sure her mistress was absorbed in her work, Minette wandered down to the meadow below. Soon the sun would burn the dew off the grass, but for now it felt wonderful on her paws. In her mind, she composed her own poem.

Cool wet on my feet
sun has not burned off the dew
much to my delight.

Unlike Madame Reveuse, whose poems tended toward long and rambling, Minette preferred the spare simplicity of haiku.

Minette's long, perfectly tapered snout twitched. Her wet, black nostrils flared. The breeze carried a new scent up from the willow cove, something she had not encountered before. A doglike smell, but not quite.

Slowly, she made her way along the edge of the meadow, nose working its way over bushes and hedges and stones. Here was Astro's mark, left two days before. And there, close to the grass, was Roxie the tiny Yorkshire terrier's mark from yesterday.

She ignored the yips and barks of the other dogs playing fetch with their people. She ignored the crow who called from a nearby tree, "Dog! Dog!" The smell grew stronger.

Minette followed her nose to a tangle of bushes and vines surrounded by large stones.

There.

She bent down and peered into the den. Inside, curled together, were a coyote and an opossum. And littering their small den were banana peels, bones, apple cores, and the fur of a former squirrel.

"Oh!" she exclaimed.

Trouble's eyes flew open.

There before him was the most beautiful creature he'd ever seen. Wide brown eyes, long neck, aristocratic snout, and, most extraordinary of all, curls! Who could have ever imagined such a thing?

Trouble sat up and grinned his best coyote grin. "Hello!" he said. "I'm Trouble."

Catching the thick odor of blood on his breath, Minette growled, "Of that I am quite certain."

She wheeled and, in a most dignified manner, trotted back up the hill to her poet.

"There you are, *ma chérie*," the poet cooed to the dog as she packed up her paper and pen. "I don't know about you, but I have worked up an appetite. Shall we go?"

While Madame retied her wide straw hat, Minette gazed down to the meadow. There, just there, she could see Trouble's head poking out from the den, watching her. With a swift, dainty squat, the poodle left her mark, then trotted away.

19

Close Encounter

Trouble watched from the cover of his den and waited. He wanted so very much to dash up to the bench where Minette had left her mark so he could read about her. Twice, he'd started creeping from the den, despite the dogs and humans still playing in the meadow. Twice, Mischief had squawked, "Don't!"

Finally, as the sun reached the tops of the trees and the summer air grew warm and thick, the humans and dogs left.

Trouble trotted up the rise to the bench and sniffed. Yes, the remarkable creature was a dog and a female. He closed his eyes and drank in her scent mark. She was not a pup, but neither was she old. She was healthy and had eaten an egg recently. Her mark said the bench and, most important, the Maker on the bench were hers and hers alone.

Trouble sniffed the bench (the Maker was female, old but healthy) and all around it. He sniffed the sidewalk for the dog's tracks and followed them all the way to Bow Bridge. Just as he was about to step onto the bridge, he heard light footsteps behind him.

He wheeled, then froze. There before him stood a small female Maker, her mouth agape and her sky-blue eyes round with wonder. She did not smell afraid, nor did she smell dangerous. As a matter of fact, Trouble thought, she smelled just the way he'd felt that first time he saw the Maker riding atop the Beast: astonished.

She took one step forward. "Hi," she said.

The spell was broken. Trouble turned and raced across the bridge, Mischief flying just above him. Between one breath and the next, the coyote pup disappeared into the thick undergrowth like a ghost.

Amelia brushed one shaking hand across her bangs and let out a long breath she hadn't realized she'd been holding. Could the coyote have been the source of the howling she'd heard the night before?

She sat on a wooden bench and slid off her backpack. She reached in, felt past her binoculars, granola bar, water bottle, bird identification book, Junior Explorers Club notebook and pencil, until her fingers found what she was looking for. She pulled out her dog-eared copy of *Peterson Field Guide to Mammals of New York*. She flipped through the pages until she came to it: a photograph labeled The Eastern Coyote. There was no mistaking those tall, pointed ears, stilt-like legs, and, most astonishing, the piercing amber eyes.

"A coyote," she said aloud. "A coyote right here in New York City!"

Amelia mulled over the implications. How would the presence of such a predator affect the natural, harmonious balance of life in Central Park? She knew the park was home to an abundance of creatures besides squirrels and pigeons. She even had a list in her notebook of all the wildlife she had seen: raccoons, skunks, chipmunks, herons, turtles, and once, on a morning she would never forget, a fox. But a coyote? Where had it come from?

Amelia took out her Junior Explorers Club notebook. She flipped past her sketches and descriptions of the birds and animals she had seen in the park until she came to a blank page. At the top, in her best handwriting, she wrote EASTERN COYOTE. She shivered with excitement at the words. Then, carefully and with striking accuracy, she drew a picture of Trouble.

When she finished, Amelia took the granola bar from her pack, peeled back the wrapping, and opened her mouth to take a bite. Then she stopped. What if the coyote was hungry? It did, after all, look rather young and scrawny. Perhaps it didn't know how to hunt yet.

She broke the bar in half, crossed the bridge, and left one half of the bar just inside the thicket of green where the coyote had disappeared. She sat beneath a cherry tree a few feet away and waited. The coyote did not reappear.

Finally, Amelia packed up her things and shouldered her pack. She looked at her Junior Explorers Club watch. Her mother would be wondering where she was.

With one last look at the thick wall of green beneath which the coyote had slipped away, she said, "I'll be back, coyote."

Trouble listened to the light footsteps of the girl fade away. He crept from beneath the tangle of ivy and sniffed doubtfully at the granola bar. It did not have the warm, rich scent of mice or voles or rabbits. It did not smell of blood, but it did smell sweet. He took one small nibble and then another. He tossed the last bite up in the air, pounced on it, and gulped it down.

20

Trouble with Swans

Later that day, after a sudden rainstorm had chased most of the humans from the park, Trouble investigated overturned boats on the lakeshore. These too smelled of Makers, but they also smelled of lily pads and ducks and fish and grass.

"What do the Makers use these for?" he wondered aloud.

"*Humans* ride in them, out into the water," Mischief explained. He snatched a worm crawling across the boat's wooden hull.

"But why?" Trouble asked.

Mischief shrugged. "I don't think they can swim."

Trouble wagged his tail. Swimming sounded like a very good idea.

He waded into the cool water until his feet left the sandy bottom and began to paddle. His bushy tail streamed out behind like a rudder. Trouble had never been in water deep enough to require swimming. Once he got used to the feeling, it felt like flying.

Mischief watched the coyote from the top of the boathouse. He had rarely spent any time worth mentioning in The Ramble. For a crow like him, it was boring. Not enough action. Not enough possibilities, like in the city.

Then he spotted the swans.

Two large, white swans sailed majestically through a rippling patch of water lilies, necks arched. He could hear them gossiping in their high, nasal voices about the family of egrets who lived beside the boat dock.

"They're just tacky," the larger of the swans said. "No manners at all."

"And their children!" the other swan gabbled. "Little hooligans, running amok!"

"Mean birds," Mischief muttered. "I'll give you something to talk about."

"Hey," he called out to Trouble. "See those big white birds out there?"

Trouble, who had just paddled back to shallow water, looked in the direction the crow pointed. He gasped. Never had he seen birds so big! Birds so white! Birds so, so . . . resplendent!

"They're very friendly," Mischief said, trying hard to sound sincere, something he had little practice with.

Trouble watched as the magnificent birds glided closer. "Really?"

"Sure," Mischief said. "I think you should swim out and"—he tried to keep the glee from his voice—"you know, introduce yourself." He watched the pup wade a little deeper into the water, his eyes fixed on the swans. He fluffed his feathers. This should liven things up.

He sidled over to the coyote. "I bet they've never met a real live coyote before. They'll be curious."

Trouble, of course, knew all about curious.

Trouble struck out for the swans. The swans watched the coyote swimming toward them.

"Who goes there?" the larger swan honked.

"I'm Trouble," the coyote answered. "I'm a real live coyote."

The smaller swan hissed. Although she had lived all her life in Central Park, she had heard about coyotes from migrating geese. She knew they were nothing but troublesome scavengers not above raiding nests.

"You," she said, beating her wide wings and standing as tall as she could, "do not belong here. Leave our water at once!"

Mischief chortled from his perch. This was going to be good.

"But," Trouble said, swimming closer to the swans, "I just came over to say hi. Where I come from, we don't have birds like you."

The larger bird, especially vain even for a swan, arched his neck and fluffed his smooth, white feathers. "Pity," he clucked.

Trouble was growing tired but decided to swim just a little closer to get a better look.

A little too close.

A long neck shot out, as quick as a snake, and pecked Trouble right on the top of his head.

"Ow!"

"Stay back, you ruffian," the larger swan hissed.

"But—" Trouble said.

The female slammed her bill against the side of Trouble's head; the male grabbed the end of Trouble's nose.

"Ow! Yow! Yow!" the coyote yipped, which was very difficult with a swan holding his nose.

Trouble tried to pull away from the swan. She beat him about the head with her wings, churning the water to a white froth.

Even Mischief had to admit this was getting out of hand. He had never meant for the coyote to get hurt.

He swooped out over the water and snatched at the top of the swan's head with his claws. "Who you calling a ruffian?" he cawed.

The swan released Trouble's nose and swiped at the crow with his wide wings. "Low-life!"

Trouble paddled frantically away from the swans. His ears rang. His nose felt as if it had been stung by a million hornets. Why had he listened to Mischief?

The swans sailed after the coyote. "We're not done with the likes of you," they honked.

Trouble swam faster.

"You'll change your name from Trouble to Sorry," the male trumpeted.

Just as he stretched his neck out and grabbed the end of Trouble's tail, Mischief streaked downward from the sky like a black arrow.

"Let him go!" he screamed.

The swan released Trouble's tail and lurched up with surprising strength. With one powerful beat of his wings, he knocked Mischief from the sky and into the water.

Trouble's paws had once again touched the sandy bottom of the lakeshore when he heard, *Crawk!*

He turned to see Mischief slapped from the sky and into the lake. *Good,* he thought. *Let him see what it's like.*

He watched for the crow to rise from the water. He did not.

He waited for the crow to shout insults at the swans. He did not.

The crow lay stunned, floating in the water, his wings spread wide. The swans pecked the crow once, then twice.

"Well done," they said in unison, and paddled away.

Despite all the trouble Mischief had caused—what with the chasing, the dive-bombing, not to mention the elevator incident—the pup would not turn his back on the crow.

Because the coyote knew that despite the crow's penchant for pranks, he had also saved him from being caught by Makers more than once. Coyotes are nothing if not fair-minded.

Trouble shook as much water from his coat as he could and swam out to the crow. Gently, he took the bird in his mouth, swam back to shore, and dropped him on the grass.

He poked Mischief with his nose. "Wake up," he said.

The bedraggled bird did not awaken.

Trouble picked up the crow by his tail feathers and gave him a good, hard shake.

Ack! Gack! Gack! the crow coughed.

Trouble dropped Mischief onto the grass, none too gently.

"Hey, careful," Mischief snapped.

"We're even now," Trouble said.

The crow shook the water from his feathers. "What's that supposed to mean?"

"You said you'd saved me," he reminded Mischief. "Now I've saved you."

"So?"

"So," Trouble said. "We're even now."

"Oh, come on," Mischief said. "I was just having a little fun."

"You call that 'fun'?" Trouble growled. "Where I come from, we don't treat our friends that way."

"I might have gone a little too far," Mischief admitted, "but—"

Trouble ignored him. "And let's not forget the 'fun' I had in the elevator."

Trouble trotted a few paces away from the crow. "I'm done with you. You're not my friend anymore."

"Ha!" Mischief called. "You need me! You'll never find that produce truck without me!"

Trouble paused. The crow might be right, he knew.

"I'll figure it out," he said, with all the confidence he did not have.

"Fine!" Mischief cawed.

"Fine!" Trouble barked.

And with that, the coyote disappeared into the fringe of ferns bordering the thick green undergrowth; the still-dripping crow lifted into the sky.

Trouble lay curled in his den. Rosebud cleaned his coat and comforted his swollen nose.

"I don't know why you ever trusted that crow," Rosebud said with a cluck of her tongue. "Everyone knows crows are tricksters, not to mention smart alecks."

"I never paid any attention to crows back in our forest. They were just like the rest of the birds—except eagles," Trouble said with a shudder. "Eagles are very worrisome. Crows you never have to think about."

Trouble sighed. "Everything is so confusing here. Pranking crows, screaming Makers, and Beasts everywhere." The pup shivered. "I've seen all I ever want to see of what's beyond. I just want to go home."

Rosebud curled close to the young coyote, even though he was wet and smelly. Quietly, she hummed songs her mother used to sing when she and her brothers and sisters lived snug and safe in her pouch.

"I want to play with my big brother, Twist, and race my sister Swift in our meadow." His eyes began to droop. Rosebud continued to hum.

"I want to hear Singing Creek and listen to my father tell my mother how beautiful she is, beautiful as the moon." His eyes closed.

"My sister Star has the best singing voice, and my brother, Pounce, is a mighty hunter." His voice trailed off, and soon he was asleep.

Rosebud continued to hum while the coyote slept. She wondered where her family was. She had not seen her mother or her ten siblings in a very long time and knew she'd never see them again. That's the way it was with opossums: families did not stay together.

The opossum pushed in closer to the curve of the coyote's belly, a place beginning to feel like home—closed her eyes, and dreamed.

21

High Jinks and Shenanigans

The next night, Trouble and Rosebud again met the fox and the owl in the glen. Clouds scudded across the moon, resting on its back in the night sky. Mischief was nowhere to be seen.

After Trouble had finished telling his story of the painful encounter with the swans and Mischief's part in it, the fox said, "Oh well, that's just like a crow, isn't it? They think they're such clever creatures, but *really*." She sniffed and gave her brushy tail a good swish.

"And don't get me started on swans," the owl said. "Such pompous birds." He tossed the mouse he clutched in his talons into his mouth and gulped it down whole, headfirst.

"Where I come from," Trouble said, "we don't have swans, and the crows mind their own business."

The fox nosed a tennis ball left behind by a forgetful dog. "Sounds a tad boring."

"I think it sounds wonderfully peaceful," Rosebud said. "No dogs to chase you, no humans calling you insulting, hurtful names like 'vermin,' 'rodent,' and"— she wiped at a tear in the corner of her black-button eyes—"'icky.'"

The fox wagged the white tip of her tail in sympathy. "I know just how you feel, my dear. Humans have no idea of the special beauty of a possum, or a fox for that matter."

Rosebud moved just a little closer to the fox.

The owl cleared his throat. "Our small friend is an *opossum*, not a possum, and a much maligned and misunderstood creature at that." For the next five minutes, the owl expounded on the difference between opossums and possums (one lives in the Americas and the other lives in Australia) and their many virtues (timid, clean, eat cockroaches and ticks).

Rosebud's nose turned deep pink with pleasure.

"My goodness," the fox said. "How do you know so much?"

The owl puffed out his chest. "I once domiciled in a wildlife refuge and attended lectures. I have superior hearing and memory."

"Why, you're a regular professor, aren't you?" the fox barked with delight.

Trouble jumped to his feet. "Hey Professor," he barked. "Since you know so much, you should be able to figure out how I can get back home."

All the creatures sitting there in the moonlight looked up at the owl. The crickets stopped singing; the frogs fell silent.

"Oh, could you?" Rosebud asked.

"Well now," the owl stammered, "in theory that is true, but then again it is a matter of orientation, triangulation, kilometers versus—"

"But will you *try*?" Trouble pleaded. "I miss my family so. My mother must be crazy with worry by now."

"You *must* try," Rosebud said to the owl.

They waited for the owl's reply as he tapped his talons on the branch. Finally, he clicked his beak in irritation. "Yes, I will try. Of course I will try." He stretched his wings in preparation of flight. "I would hardly be an owl worthy of the species if I did not apply my considerable intellect to—"

"Hurray!" Trouble yipped. "Thank you, Professor!"

He picked up the fox's tennis ball in his mouth. It tasted of the dog who had left it behind.

Trouble flung the ball in the air. He watched with amazement as it rolled down the gentle slope to the pond. "Moon and stars," he barked in wonder. "How does it run without legs?"

"It's a ball, silly," the fox said. "Don't you have balls where you come from?"

Trouble shook his head. "Is it to eat?"

"Better than that," the fox said, galloping down to the ball, "it's a toy."

Trouble cocked his head to one side.

The fox picked up the ball in her mouth, tossed it in the air, and caught it. "It's to play with!"

"Oh, play!" Trouble dropped to his elbows, stuck his rear end in the air, and wagged his tail.

The fox tossed the ball to the coyote, who scooped it up in his mouth.

Trouble tossed the ball to Rosebud, who tossed it back to the coyote. Trouble flipped it toward the fox. The fox caught it and, with a gleeful bark, ran into the forest.

"Hey!" Trouble barked.

Trouble raced after the fox, chasing the white tip of her tail. The fox slowed just enough to let the coyote think he could catch her and then off she dashed again.

Trouble intercepted the fox, grabbed the ball, and raced around and around a tree.

Rosebud grinned with delight; the owl turned

his back on the whole nonsense. "Whoever saw such high jinks," he muttered. "Most undignified, all this cavorting and shenanigans.

"Whoever heard of a member of the Opossum Clan and Coyote Clan being friends," the owl sniffed. "It is not the natural order of things."

"I've never heard of an opossum and a fox being friends," Rosebud pointed out.

"Not even here, in the city?" Trouble asked as he flopped down next to Rosebud. He thought about all the things in this city of Makers that made no sense.

They shook their heads. "Not even here," the owl said.

"We are friends because of *you*," Rosebud said.

"And the better for it," the fox added.

Unbeknownst to the friends, the crow watched from high atop the tall pine at the edge of the glen. Mischief had heard all the talk too, including the parts about himself. Normally, he loved being the topic of conversation, for good and even for ill, because it was, after all, about him.

But this time a war of feelings wrestled in the crow's black breast. Feelings so heavy, he could barely lift his wings and fly away.

22

Mornings with Minette

Still, Trouble was lonely.

As the days passed, he even missed Mischief. At least the crow didn't sleep all day like Rosebud and the owl, nor did he have children to care for like the fox. And Mischief was every bit as curious as he was.

If it hadn't been for his talks with Minette, the loneliness would have been unbearable.

They met every morning in a small cove on the lake where the cattails and duck grass crowded the bank. At first they met there because it was the place where Trouble could easily keep out of sight of humans. But it didn't take long for Trouble to realize that, to most humans, he was invisible.

"They don't see things that are unexpected or out

of place," Minette explained in her melodious voice.

"Is it because of their small eyes?" Trouble asked.

Minette thought this over. Finally, she said, "Perhaps, but I think it is mostly because they are involved in their own world. Except for the children," she amended.

They talked of many things on these mornings. He told her about his family and his home beside Singing Creek. She told him about her life with the poet. She remembered very little of her puppyhood or her parents, whether she had had brothers and sisters. "My memories begin in the warm sunlight of Madame Reveuse's apartment," she said simply.

Mischief watched from his perch in a sycamore tree as the poodle trotted up the long hill to her human. She stopped once and looked back over her shoulder at Trouble, barely hidden in the hedgerow.

"Hum," Mischief said. "He's getting careless. Somebody's going to spot him and then . . ."

He gave himself a good shake. "Oh, who cares," he said. He pushed off from the branch of the sycamore tree. "Not me," he cawed. "Not me."

He flew across the park to the far north end, where, in the forked roots of an ancient oak tree, his treasures lay hidden.

He plucked the curtain of twigs and pine needles

aside and gazed on his wealth: buttons, coins, candy wrappers, marbles, watches, rings, shiny strings of colorful beads, a tiny plastic car, a baby's rattle, a driver's license (with a most unflattering picture), sunglasses, and, most recently, Vera Trumpowski's ring of keys.

But today, his bounty brought him very little pleasure. His mind kept returning to other things— Trouble to be exact.

Trouble telling Minette he was forgetting what home is. Trouble laughing and playing on moonlit nights in the glen with the fox and the owl, and that possum.

"Oh, excuse me," Mischief said aloud. "I meant *opossum*.

"Who cares?" The crow covered his treasures and lit out for the city.

It certainly wasn't because he cared about that crazy coyote that he flew back to the place where they'd first met.

And it certainly wasn't because he cared that he spent day after day watching the fresh-produce truck Trouble had stowed away in. Noting how it came at the same time every other morning and left late in the afternoon. Noting that the female driver was very careful but the male driver was not. And before long, Mischief knew which days the female driver stepped out of the truck cab and which days the male driver did.

Not that Mischief cared. He was just—curious.

And so we shall say that it was curiosity, not caring, that propelled Mischief up into the sky one afternoon to follow the fresh-produce truck away from the city.

23

Hiding in Plain Sight

Mischief had been right: Trouble was becoming careless.

As soon as the poet and the poodle claimed their usual bench, Trouble stopped whatever he was doing, barely bothering to keep out of sight. After all, it did seem to be as Minette had said: humans did not see the unexpected, especially when they held the small square things in their hands and against their heads. He reckoned he had been in the park for over seven moons now, and not a single human had noticed him except that young human. She was just a pup, though. And Vetch? Trouble's worries about him disappeared with his dreams.

But the poet saw. Like all artists, she looked for the unexpected. Her inspiration came from small miracles. Like the unexpected miracle of a coyote in Central Park.

Madame Reveuse unclipped the poodle's leash and gave her a parting pat. She watched bemused as her elegant Minette gamboled on the green grass and splashed along the bank of the lake with an uncharacteristic frivolity.

Trouble watched a fish swim lazily along the edge of the lake. He had given Minette a frog once, and several fat mice, but she had politely declined to eat them. Perhaps a fish.

He crouched low and gathered his hind legs beneath him.

Just a little closer, a little closer . . . Trouble pounced! He thrust his long coyote snout under the water and, before the fish knew what it was about, grabbed it and flung it onto the grass.

Minette watched as the fish flipped and flopped.

"Eat it," Trouble urged. "You'll love it."

Minette placed one paw on the fish and regarded it mournfully as it gasped for air. Really, this was absurd. She knew Trouble meant well, but still . . .

Gently, she picked up the fish and placed it back in the pond. She watched as it floated, stunned, then darted away in jubilant panic.

Trouble sighed. "Aw, come on, Minette. That was a fish. Do you know how hard they are to catch?"

Minette gave him an affectionate nuzzle. "My friend, that fish needs to live more than I need to eat. Madame feeds me well."

"It's not the same," Trouble pouted. "It's wild."

Changing the subject, Minette asked, "Has the Professor found anything to help you find your way home?"

"No," he replied. "Not yet, but that's okay."

"You don't sound particularly unhappy about that—not like you used to," Minette pointed out.

Trouble nosed a round plastic disk he had seen some of the dogs playing with. Perhaps he would take it back to Rosebud. She always found such clever uses for the things he found.

"It's not so bad here," he replied. "There's plenty of food, and it's easier to find than back in the woods."

"Yes but—"

"And there are so many curious things." Just the night before, the fox had introduced him to the fun of sprinklers.

"Don't you get lonely?" Minette asked, her eyes full of concern.

"Lonely? I have Rosebud and owl, and fox, and

you," he said with a shy, low wag of his tail. "Back home, I didn't really have friends." He could imagine what his mother would say if he had made friends with a fox, much less an opossum. He could hear his mother's voice say "You cannot be friends with members of one of *those* clans! It's just not done!"

"But what about the moon?" the poodle asked.

"What about it?"

"I never hear you sing to it at night anymore."

Trouble considered this. It was true that he had not howled his moon song in many nights, but he had found other things to do with his friends.

"Rosebud and owl don't sing moon songs," he said. "Even the fox doesn't pay that much attention to it," which, in all honesty, Trouble found rather odd.

"Besides," he said, "Rosebud is afraid of the full moonlight." Although, with the help of her friends, she was becoming less afraid.

"Well," Minette said, standing and stretching. "I for one miss hearing you sing at night."

Trouble gazed adoringly at the apricot-colored poodle with the ring of sparkling stars encircling her long, graceful neck. "If it will make you happy to hear me sing at night, I will sing," he said.

Minette trotted across the glen and scrambled up the rock, Trouble on her heels. She stopped beside her poet, napping in the morning sun, and nudged her hand.

The old woman's eyes opened. Blue eyes met yellow eyes. "Ah, *bonjour, mon ami*." The old woman held out her hand.

Trouble took one step forward. His heart pounded. This was a Human, after all. He heard his mother's voice growl, "Nothing good comes from Makers."

Trouble whirled and raced down the apron of stone, past the girl Amelia following the trill of a song sparrow, and into the bracken. "Listen tonight," he yipped to Minette. "Listen!"

That night, when the moon rose and settled in the eastern sky, Minette heard Trouble sing. But the song was not about Mother Moon. Nor did he sing about missing his home. The song he sang this night was about her.

> *You are my moon, you are my star.*
> *I will stay beside you*
> *and never stray far.*
> *I will never forget*
> *my friend Minette.*
> *My friend Minette.*

The owl groaned. "You sound like a besotted schoolboy rather than *Canis latrans*."

The fox sighed wistfully. "I thought it was perfectly lovely."

Rosebud studied Trouble as she munched on a mealworm. He had changed, and the changes worried her. The cloak of wildness that had clung to him, that had informed his every move, was fading.

"You are becoming like us," she said, her eyes glittering.

"So," Trouble said.

"What's wrong with that?" the fox asked.

"There's everything wrong with that," Rosebud snapped. "He's *not* one of us, can never *be* one of us."

Trouble shifted uncomfortably. "But . . ."

Rosebud marched right up to Trouble and gave him a stern nip on his leg.

"Ow!" he yipped. "What was that for?"

"That," she snarled, "was to remind you of that human, Officer Vetch. Have you forgotten how dangerous he is?"

Trouble yawned. "I bet he's forgotten all about me."

"I bet he *hasn't* forgotten about you," Rosebud said in a gentler voice. "If he catches you, you'll never be wild again."

Trouble snorted. "Even humans can't make something that's wild *un*wild."

The owl and the fox exchanged a look of fear. "I'm

afraid, dear, they can," the fox said.

"How?" Trouble asked. "Besides kill me, that is," he added.

"There is that," the owl conceded, "but there is something worse."

Trouble's rust-colored brows pulled together in puzzlement. "What?"

"Follow me," the owl said. He pushed off the branch and sailed as silent as a ghost into the night.

24

The Place
of the Once Wild

Trouble followed the wide wings of the owl south.
They skirted The Sheep Meadow, littered
with balls, Frisbees, plastic bags, soda cans, water bot-
tles, plastic wrappers, cigarette butts (which had made
Trouble very sick when he'd eaten one), several blan-
kets, and a pair of plastic shoes.

Sprinklers sprang to life, sending great arcs of
water raining down on the parched grass. Trouble
paused. Oh, how he loved playing with the fox in the
sprinklers!

"Come!" the owl hooted from above.

Trouble sighed. He loped after the shadow of the
owl rippling on the grass, then on the sidewalk in front
of him.

They veered east. Although few humans visited the park this late at night, Trouble was still wild enough to stay just out of reach of the light cast by the row of streetlamps.

A curious breeze scudded up from the south. Trouble stopped in his tracks. He lifted his head and searched the breeze, his black nose sorting familiar scents from unfamiliar.

Here he smelled the familiar deep, sweet smell of an unemptied garbage can, the acrid smell of the day's heat still trapped in the sidewalk, and always, the salty, sickly smell of humans everywhere.

But there—just there, and not far beyond—a smell that pinned his tall ears flat against his head, a smell that tucked his tail between his legs. He smelled fear, boredom, outrage, a vague scent of menace, and worst of all, despair.

Trouble whined. He looked back the way they had come.

"This way," the owl barked. Trouble knew better than to argue.

The smells grew stronger, scents of furred and feathered.

Trouble stopped. He pricked his ears forward and listened beyond the night sounds—the piping of bats, the rustle of leaves, the chirp of crickets, the never-ending hum and bleat of traffic—he'd grown accustomed to.

Beyond those sounds he heard mutterings, grumblings, rumblings, and whimperings from many unfamiliar, overlapping voices. "If only," and "How I wish," and "Once upon a time," and "Just once I'd like to. . . .". Trouble knew that feeling all too well. His curiosity won over fear.

A light rain began to fall. Trouble galloped after the owl until they arrived at the tall gates of the Central Park Zoo.

Had anyone passed by the gates of the Central Park Zoo that night, they would have seen this: a young, tawny coyote with improbably long legs and a bushy, black-tipped tail slip through the gap between the bars of the tall iron gates. The only witnesses to this remarkable sight were a great horned owl and the moon.

"This way," the owl hooted as he winged low over the zoo.

Trouble held tight to the owl's shadow as he trotted past sleeping polar bears and snow monkeys, a giant anteater and a banded mongoose. Snow leopards watched the coyote's passing with aloof light-green eyes. Sea lions slapped their flippers together in applause at the sight of this surprise. Peacocks and puffins agreed that something was up in the zoo.

"Eleven point two more lengths," the owl called.

Trouble didn't know how much more of this his keen sense of smell could take—the overwhelming smell of rotting food, the body waste of so many different animals. The smell of hopelessness. And most puzzling of all, everywhere among this extraordinary collection of wild creatures, the sour scent of humans.

They rounded a bend in the trail. Trouble skidded to a stop and gasped.

There, standing in the moonlight in his own enclosure, was a wolf. He was tall, twice the height of Trouble's father, and broad in the chest. His fur shimmered silver and black in the moonlight.

Trouble had heard many stories from his parents about their larger cousins, the Wolf Clan. He couldn't imagine a being so noble and wild living here. Not without a fight, anyway.

"Greetings, little cousin," the wolf barked.

Trouble lowered his haunches and turned his head away from the wolf in supplication. He wagged the very tip of his tail.

"Greetings," he whined. "I am honored to meet you."

The wolf limped over to the thick plexiglass partition keeping him in and the world out. He studied the coyote pup cowering at his feet.

"How did you get in here?" he asked.

"I followed the owl," Trouble said, lifting his chin to the bird gazing down on them. "He wanted to show me something."

The wolf snorted. "Nothing much here to see except all of us Once Wilds living out our days being gawked at by humans." The wolf spat the last word with disgust.

"How long have you been here?" Trouble asked.

The wolf yawned. "Who knows? It all runs together after you've seen as many seasons as I have."

Trouble shivered. "Seasons?"

"Yes," the wolf said. He picked up a large beef bone and halfheartedly nibbled the meat still clinging to the bone. "I was in another place such as this before, and then I was brought here."

The wolf studied the coyote. He smelled the wild coursing through the coyote's veins. He felt his longing, his need for deep forests and cold, rushing streams and family.

"I was once wild like you," the wolf said.

A tiny glint of light shone in the wolf's eyes. "I ran forever through endless forests and across frozen lakes. Until the trap crushed my leg and the humans tried to heal me. And now this."

"Have you ever tried to escape?" Trouble asked. "To return to your home, your pack?"

Out of the shadows, a beautiful silver female wolf walked up to the wolf and nudged his shoulder with affection.

The wolf sighed. "I would not leave her, ever."

Trouble studied the small stream of water coursing through the wolf's enclosure, the scattering of logs and tree limbs, the rising cliffs that did not smell like cliffs at all. "Still, they didn't kill you," Trouble pointed out.

The light left the wolf's eyes and left them flat, dead. "There are worse things than death for those who were once wild," the wolf growled. "I would advise you to leave this city, little cousin, and go home before they catch you."

And with that, he turned his back on Trouble and limped to his den, his mate by his side.

25

The Scent of Home

The crow had flown all through the night. He was exhausted.

Crows are not migratory birds. They do not fly long distances like geese and hummingbirds. Crows are stop-and-go birds, certainly not used to flying over eighty miles. Every part of Mischief hurt.

As he flapped his weary, rain-sodden wings, he thought not about the long flight following the fresh-produce truck away from the city, over a wide river, and above more trees than he ever imagined existed in the world—no, he thought about Trouble's family and the promise he had made to Trouble's heartbro-ken mother: he, Mischief, would do his very best to bring Trouble back home to her.

Finally, he saw beneath his wings the vast green of Central Park. "Thank Crow," he croaked. He spiraled down to the sycamore tree and called for Trouble.

Mischief called and called his name until his voice became hoarse. He fluttered down to the den of Trouble and Rosebud and walked inside. Rain dripped onto the matt of grass and leaves. A Frisbee, tennis balls, a squirrel's tail, a plastic water bottle, and a black rubber boot littered the spacious den. But no Trouble or Rosebud. The coyote and opossum had most likely, he reckoned, sought someplace drier. Judging by the smell, though, they'd be back.

"Nothing for it but to watch and wait."

Thunder cracked. The rain came down harder.

Suddenly, the rubber boot moved just the tiniest bit. Mischief cocked his head to one side. He pecked the boot. It moved again. He poked his head inside and sniffed: opossum.

"Rosebud?" he called.

The boot shifted from one side to the other. A pair of shining black eyes looked out at the crow.

"Mischief?"

"Yeah," the crow answered, "it's me. Where's Trouble?"

Rosebud crawled out and frowned. "Why do you want to know?"

"I have something I need to give him, something from his family."

Her frown deepened. "His family? You expect me to believe you've somehow miraculously seen his family?"

Mischief looked down at a strip of deer hide he clutched in his claw. Trouble's older brother, Twist, had given it to him to remind Trouble of home. Mischief would forever remember how each member of the Singing Creek Pack had solemnly rubbed their scent on the strip of hide. "Yes," he said. "I have."

Rosebud swiveled her dappled ears. "I'm listening."

And so it was that the crow and the opossum passed that rainy summer morning, one weaving an improbable (but true) story and the other listening with growing wonder.

Mischief told her about all the things he had seen beneath his wings: the tidy pastures dotted with cows and horses, the white clapboard house where the fresh-produce truck finally—finally!—stopped, the cornfields and gardens and the wild forest beyond. He told her about the cliffs and old apple orchards, the sound of Singing Creek, and the meadow, just as Trouble had described it.

And the pack, howling the loneliest, saddest song he'd ever heard.

"I've never been big on family myself," Mischief said, "but you can't believe how much they love him and miss him. They need him too," he added.

Rosebud nodded. "Trouble needs his home, and home is not here."

"He's been away from the wild too long," Mischief said. "He's getting careless."

"He thinks he can live here among humans and still be Wildborn," Rosebud agreed.

"He's not like us," Mischief said. "Once they know he's here, humans will never allow something that wild to just be."

Rosebud had to trust the crow. "He's most likely at that boathouse. He likes to go there when it rains like this."

"I'll find him," Mischief promised. "I'll bring him back here. Then we have to figure out how to get him home."

Trouble watched the rainfall. He raised his face to the sky and felt the cool, wet drops pepper his muzzle and ears. For a moment he was back in the woods with his family, who loved the rain too. He and Twist had had many wild games of chase and keep-away in the rain. Here, no one except the ducks came out during a storm, not even the squirrels.

He wondered what the animals in the Place of the Once Wild were doing on this rainy morning. His heart trembled as he remembered the dullness in the wolf's eyes. There had been no spirit in him. No wild smell.

Still, he thought as he nosed the lid off a garbage can, what were the chances he'd get caught?

"Oh well," he consoled himself, "at least here no one tells me to shake the mud from my coat before I come into the den."

Trouble had just pulled a tasty bone from the trash bin outside the boathouse when he heard, "Hey! Trouble!"

The pup looked up and saw Mischief perched under the eaves of the boathouse. Something brown and limp dangled from his beak.

He narrowed his eyes. "What do you want?"

Mischief set down the strip of deer hide. "I brought you something."

Trouble snorted. "Yeah, and what's it going to do? Set my mouth on fire?" He picked up the bone, turned his back on the crow, and trotted down the wet slope to a rowboat propped on its side. He crawled under and curled up with the particularly delicious treasure.

Mischief picked up the hide, flew over to the boat, and hopped inside.

Trouble glared at the crow.

Mischief dropped the hide. "Look," he said. "I know I got a little carried away playing jokes and all."

"You got that right," Trouble growled.

"I'm sorry, Trouble, I really am," Mischief said, and he really and truly was.

Trouble eyed the deer hide. "So what's that?"

"I found your family," Mischief said. "And they sent this to you."

Trouble's heart stopped. The hair along his spine rose. "You did what? How?"

Mischief relayed the story once again of his curiosity, his long flight, and his encounter with the Singing Creek Pack. "Curiosity can take you a long way," the crow concluded.

Trouble bent his nose to the deer hide.

A symphony of smells rose up from the hide. He inhaled and, on that breath, the scent of home raced into his nostrils and into his coyote mind.

He smelled the damp earth of the den where he had lived with his brother and sisters safe in the warmth of their mother's side. He smelled the meadow where he and Twist played and his brother Pounce hunted. Where he raced his sister Swift, and where he listened to his sister Star sing to the moon and beyond.

The rain stopped. The sun broke through the

clouds, and birds sang their thanks.

Trouble crawled from beneath the overturned boat and gazed out across the lake. Tiny ponds of rain lay cupped in lily pads; steam rose from the sidewalk above, creating a peculiar beauty Trouble never tired of. Soon, he knew, the humans would appear in great numbers with their loud voices, sour-salty smell, and never-ending fascinations. Later, from his boulder above the willow-ringed cove, he'd watch turtles bask in the sun.

Somewhere, a door slammed. Voices drifted across the lake, not so far away. Mischief noted that the coyote did not startle and slink away at the sounds like he used to. Instead, the pup threw his ears forward with curiosity.

The crow's heart sank.

"It's time for you to go home, Trouble," he said.

"Maybe I like it here," said Trouble, sniffing the bone. "Finding food is easier than back in the wild. I can do whatever I want, and I have friends—real friends—like you and Rosebud and the Professor and the fox and—"

"And that dog," Mischief interrupted.

If a coyote could blush, Trouble's face would have been as red as a ripe berry. Instead, he looked away. "Her name is Minette."

It took all the crow's self-control not to make a smart-aleck remark; instead, he said, "But she's not a coyote, Trouble. She's not *wild* like you."

"You're wild, aren't you?" Trouble snapped. "And Rosebud, and the fox too. You live here just fine, so why can't I?"

"It's not the same!" Mischief cawed in frustration. "*We're* not the same as you!"

But Trouble didn't listen. Instead, he turned his back on the crow and slipped into the mist rising from the lake.

26

The Plan

That night, the friends gathered as they always did in the moonlit glen. For the third (and he truly hoped the last) time, Mischief told the story of finding Trouble's family.

"Trouble must go back to his family," Rosebud said. "And the sooner the better."

All eyes turned to the coyote pup.

Trouble studied the night sky. When he'd first come to the city, the moon had been a thin crescent. By his reckoning, the moon had risen twelve nights since then. The full moon was just days away.

"I'm not sure I want to go back," Trouble confessed.

"Trouble." Rosebud sighed in exasperation.

"Did you learn nothing from our visit to the zoo?" the Professor asked.

Mischief picked up the deer hide, hopped over to the coyote, and dropped it at Trouble's feet. "They miss you, Trouble."

Trouble sniffed the hide again. Yes, he smelled the safety of the den beneath the roots of an old oak tree and the comforting scent of his brother and sisters. He smelled the lessons he'd learned from his father, lessons in patience and respect—and family.

And then he smelled his mother, a grief-yearning scent, thick with heartbreak and hope. It was home. It was him. Everything he was and would become.

Trouble blinked and shook his head as if waking from a long dream. "How could I have forgotten?" he asked.

"I've been gone too long," he said. "I need to go home."

The fox's dark eyes glittered in the moonlight. "Of course you do, my friend," she said.

"How?" the owl hooted from above.

"I have a plan all figured out," Mischief said.

Mischief had had a lot of time to think about how to return Trouble to his family during his flight back to the city. And, except for a hole here and there, he thought it was a pretty good plan.

"Like you said, Professor," Mischief said, "the only way for Trouble to get back home is the way he came: in the fresh-produce truck."

"That seems easy enough," the owl said.

"Except it's on the other side of the city and," he said, "we didn't exactly take the most direct route here."

"Do you remember the way back to where you arrived in the city?" Rosebud asked Trouble.

Trouble frowned. It was all a jumble of screeching, angry humans, blaring car horns, elevators, twisting side streets, subway trains, and, worst of all, Officer Vetch.

"Not really," he said, "and I can't find the North Star in this city sky."

"If he could fly, it would be much easier," the owl muttered. Which just proved, he thought not for the first time, the superiority of the Winged Clan.

"Yes but," Mischief said with excitement, "he *can* ride a subway train."

"But we didn't ride the train very far," Trouble pointed out. "At least I don't think we did."

"Right, but there has to be a train that goes across the city, from here to there," Mischief said.

"So we just need to figure out which train will take us across the city, get Trouble back on the truck on the day it comes into the city, and on his way home," Mischief said.

"Without getting caught," Rosebud added.

"That doesn't sound too hard," Trouble said.

"It won't be if the Professor will help me," Mischief said.

"If you're such a clever bird, why do you need me?" The owl sniffed.

"Because you're a raptor," Mischief said with a humbleness unfamiliar to him. "Your hearing and sight are a million times better than mine.

"I can plan, I can scheme, but you can calculate. We not only have to know which trains go where, but exactly how far it is and how long it will take. Timing," he said, "will be everything. And," Mischief added, "we have to do this at night when there are fewer humans."

When he finished, the animals looked up at the owl. "Well?" Rosebud asked, twisting the deer hide in her hands. "What do you think?"

Finally, the owl twitched his feathered, horned tufts. "Although it lacks a certain elegance in design and is most assuredly the work of a less-than-sophisticated mind—"

Everyone held their breath.

"It could work," the Professor concluded.

"And you'll help?" Trouble asked.

"It certainly has no hope of success without me," the owl answered.

A cheer and a whoop and a *yip, yip, yip* rose up through the trees.

"Then we need to fly across the city to the train station," Mischief said to the owl. "The sooner we get your calculations going, the sooner we can get Trouble out of danger."

27

News

The next morning, Amelia sat at the small kitchen table eating her buttered toast and thinking again about her brush with the coyote pup. He had run right past her. She could have bent down and touched him, if she'd had her wits about her. She wanted more than anything to go to Central Park and look for him. Would he still be there after almost two weeks? she wondered.

If she hurried, she could go back, search for the coyote, then be home before her mother returned from teaching dance class.

She took one last gulp of orange juice. She stood and glanced at the newspaper sitting on her father's chair. She gasped. There, at the very bottom corner of the paper, was the headline: **POSSIBLE COYOTE SIGHTINGS IN CENTRAL PARK**.

Amelia bent over the paper. Aloud she read:

"Has a wild coyote taken up residence in Central Park? Several park regulars have reported seeing a smallish, long-legged, big-eared doglike animal with piercing yellow eyes in the area of The Ramble.

"'It's a menace!' one woman told this reporter. 'It actually walked toward my dog!' 'I've seen it here before, hanging out with a poodle,' another park regular commented. 'It just seemed curious,' another had said.

"When asked to comment on the likelihood of a coyote living in the middle of one of the biggest cities in the world, Officer Ambrose Vetch of New York City Animal Control and Welfare said, 'It's not beyond the realm of possibility. Coyotes have turned up in Chicago, Seattle, and, of course, Los Angeles.' And what should be done about this coyote in New York City? 'Central Park is no place for a dangerous wild animal,' he said, 'but Central Park Zoo is. And that's exactly where we'll take that coyote once we catch him.'"

Amelia's heart pounded. "They can't take him to the zoo," she whispered in horror. Didn't they know the young coyote wasn't dangerous? Didn't they appreciate just how astonishing and wonderful it was to have a coyote living in their midst?

Amelia grabbed her pack and slung it over her shoulders. She had to come up with a plan to protect the coyote.

Minette lay on her belly, her body half in, half out of Trouble and Rosebud's den. That morning, the poet had read to her the article about the Trouble sighting. "I have rarely seen Madame so upset," the poodle said.

Rosebud's whiskers trembled. "This is terrible news, just terrible."

"Are you sure it said possible *coyote* sightings?" Trouble asked for the second time. "Maybe your human misread it. Her eyes are very small, after all."

Mischief clicked his bill. "We have to get you out of here before that Vetch finds you."

Trouble felt sick at the sound of the human's name. "Did you and the Professor figure out the trains and the timing?"

"About that," Mischief said, with a cough, "I have good news and bad news."

"What's the good news?" Trouble, ever the optimist, asked.

"You can't believe how good that owl's hearing and sight are, and how he puts that all together," Mischief said. "We had no problem finding the place where the truck comes. There's even a train stop right there."

"I sense a 'but' coming," Rosebud said.

Mischief looked away. "Yes, well the bad news is, we couldn't exactly find the train station that brought us here, the one we rode with you," he said to the opossum.

Trouble leaped to his feet. "I could find it—I know I could!"

"No!" they all cried.

"You're not going anywhere," the poodle growled.

Minette heard her madame's voice calling.

"I have to go," she said. She looked pointedly at Trouble. "*Don't* let anyone see you!"

Trouble watched miserably as Minette trotted up the hill, away from him. He knew he had to leave the city, and soon, or he'd end up like the wolf. But the thought of never seeing the poodle again made him want to howl with heartbreak.

Mischief gave him a sharp peck on his leg.

"Ow!" Trouble yipped.

"Don't even think about it," Mischief warned.

Trouble pulled his head back into the den and

plopped down with a huff. He rubbed the side of his face on the deer hide.

"I'm going to look for the Professor," Mischief said, "see if he's come up with an idea for finding that train station."

"Don't let him out of your sight," he said to Rosebud. And with a hop, hop, and flutter, the crow was gone.

Trouble sighed. "What do we do now?"

Rosebud yawned again. "I find a nap passes the time quite nicely."

Trouble circled once, then twice, and plopped down inside the den with a grunt.

Rosebud settled into the curve of the coyote's side. It was hard for her to imagine she'd ever found his rich, musky smell anything but comforting.

"Boring, boring," he muttered.

"Just sleep, Trouble, and dream of your home in the woods," the little opossum said as her eyes drooped, then closed.

Trouble lay his chin across his paws and tried his very best to ignore all the interesting sounds and smells outside their den. The clamorous barking of a dog playing with its human; the scent of humans eating something delicious down by the pond. He wondered what they'd leave behind.

He tried telling himself the stories Twist used to tell the pups to get them to sleep. The remembering made him homesick.

He tried breathing in rhythm with Rosebud, but that made him dizzy.

He tried counting squirrels, but that just made him hungry, which made him try to recall the last time he'd eaten a nice, juicy squirrel. Which made him wonder, not for the first time, how so many squirrels could live in one place.

It was no use. The den, which had always seemed so spacious, so comforting, now suffocated him.

He listened as Rosebud's breathing deepened to snuffly snores. Nothing could wake her once she started snoring.

Carefully, he stood and stretched. He'd just take a quick look outside, he thought. Find something to eat and then go back into the den before Mischief returned with the owl. No one would be the wiser.

Trouble crept out from beneath the cover of the den and blinked in the sunlight. He raised his nose and took in a deep, searching sniff. He could smell humans and hear their endless chatter in the grassy field below. The scent of the field between him and the willow cove, where he could get a nice cool drink of water and possibly a duck egg or a fat squirrel.

He glanced back at the den. Rosebud snored on.

He looked up at the sun-washed sky. No crow, no owl.

Trouble shook the worry from his coat and, with a certain jaunty trot, headed down to the cove.

28

Finding Trouble

Amelia trotted as fast as she could across Central Park. "Of course a coyote would live in The Ramble," she muttered under her breath. "It's the wildest part of the park. What kind of Junior Explorer am I not to have figured that out?"

She skirted Cherry Hill. She heard music coming from Belvedere Castle. She dodged bicycles and runners and horse-drawn carriages as she crossed the street. What would a coyote possibly think of this?

Finally, she reached the deep green of The Ramble. Trees closed overhead. A winding path bordered by a wild tangle of ivy and thick stands of blackberry bushes beckoned. She hesitated. She had never ventured from the paved confines of the park. But this was where the wild in the city lived. How could she not go?

One step, then another into the heart of The Ramble. She closed her eyes and took a deep breath. So, so quiet. She felt muscles she hadn't realized were clenched relax.

Amelia wandered through bracken and scrambled over rock outcroppings, seeing the forest as the coyote must see it. She looked for signs that might point to where in this wilderness the coyote lived.

Something caught her eye. There, pressed into a wet place in the dirt and leaves, a doglike paw print. She took off her pack, reached in, and pulled out a copy of *Animal Tracks and Signs*. She opened to the page she had already marked. There it was, an eastern coyote print. A perfect match. A chill of excitement ran up her spine.

She followed Trouble's tracks along a faint, winding trail. Through the tall birch trees, their bark paper-white, over ancient stones, and around fallen logs.

Amelia stopped to wipe the sweat from her brow. She slapped the mosquitoes on her arm and studied the collection of paw prints in the wet dirt.

She looked closer. The bramble formed a hedge-row, and there, just where she stood, barely discernable to the eye, was an opening.

Amelia dropped to her knees and looked in. She did not see the glowing yellow eyes of a coyote as she'd hoped. Instead, she saw an odd collection of bones, a squirrel's tail, apple cores, a rubber boot, feathers, tennis balls, and a Frisbee. And, lying among the treasures, snoring ever so softly, a small opossum.

Amelia reached out to touch the opossum.

Rosebud's sensitive whiskers felt the heat from the human's hand. Her eyes flew open. In that split second she understood two things: a human's hand was reaching for her, and Trouble was gone.

Rosebud squealed and hissed in alarm.

The hand jerked back. The human scrambled away.

The opossum scuttled to the opening of the den. Rosebud squinted against the sunlight. She watched with alarm as the small human followed Trouble's well-worn trail down to the cove.

Against every one of her better instincts, Rosebud followed.

29

"The Death of You"

Trouble's stomach rumbled. He'd found the duck nests empty. The heat had driven the squirrels to the cool canopy of the treetops.

He lowered his head and lapped at the water.

"Oh, there you are!"

Trouble raised his head. There, just ten tail-lengths away, stood the small human he had encountered before. How had he not heard or smelled her approach?

He crouched and looked for a way to escape. Behind him was the cove and the wide lake; in front of him, the human blocked his trail into the deep woods.

She took a step toward him. "It's okay," she said in a soft voice. "I won't hurt you."

The pup took two steps back.

Slowly, Amelia took the pack from her back and placed it on the ground. She opened the top. The delicious smell of roasted leg of lamb filled the air.

His mouth watered. He took one step, then two toward the smell.

Amelia took out the lamb leg and unwrapped it. As a Junior Explorer, she knew better than to get too close to wildlife, much less to feed it. But if she could just tame the coyote a little bit, if people could see he was not a threat, wouldn't it be worth it?

Amelia held out the meat to the coyote. "This is for you," she said. "I'm your friend, see?"

Trouble did indeed see the leg, glistening with fat.

Trouble lunged for the meat.

"Oh!" Amelia jumped back in surprise, landing on her bottom.

"Look! A coyote's attacking that little girl!"

Trouble turned toward the noise, the leg of lamb clutched in his jaws.

A group of humans walking up from the lake trail stood wide-eyed in disbelief. They pointed the small square things they always carried with them at the pup and the girl. *Click!*

A large human reached down and grabbed a rock. He hurled it at the coyote, striking him in the side.

Trouble yelped and dropped the meat.

In a panic, he ran one way and then the other.

"Get it!"

"Kill it!"

"Call the police!"

"No!" Amelia cried, scrambling to her feet. Her heart pounded in her chest. "He's friendly!"

"Trouble!" Rosebud hissed from the forest above.

The coyote darted past the girl and raced up the hill to his friend.

The last Amelia saw of Trouble was his bushy tail disappearing into the bracken, followed by the hairless tail of an opossum.

"What. Were. You. Thinking?" Rosebud punctuated each word with a poke of her pointy nose into Trouble's side. "You weren't supposed to go anywhere!"

"I was hungry," Trouble whined. "And bored. I didn't think—"

"That's right, you didn't," the opossum snapped. "Now all kinds of humans have seen you."

"Maybe they'll forget they saw me," Trouble offered. He curled up in the corner of their den and gnawed on a squirrel's tail.

Rosebud's nostrils flared with irritation. "I doubt that. They were very upset. And I can tell you from experience, Trouble, there's nothing more dangerous than angry humans!"

Just then, Trouble and Rosebud heard a flutter and a swoop. Mischief strutted into the den.

"Did you find the Professor?" Rosebud asked.

Mischief puffed up his chest feathers. "Of course I did. If there's a job to be done, just leave it to a crow."

"Oh stop." The Professor stooped, then shuffled into the den. "I can barely endure your self-aggrandizing at night. During the day, it's intolerable."

"Please," Rosebud said, worrying her tail, "you two must work together. Things have gone from bad to worse!"

Trouble noted that the nocturnal owl looked much less grand, much less intelligent really, in the daylight. His golden eyes were dim, the tufts above his ears sagged.

As if reading the coyote's mind, the owl fixed Trouble with a withering glare. "What is it now?"

Trouble looked away. "I was hungry and bored," he said by way of explanation.

Mischief groaned. "Please tell me you didn't leave the den."

"I thought you were keeping an eye on him," Mischief said to Rosebud.

"I did," she said, "until I fell asleep." She looked to

the owl for sympathy. "I just couldn't stay awake."

The owl slowly closed his eyes, muttered something none of them could understand, then said, "What happened?"

After Rosebud finished her tale of Trouble's disastrous encounter with the small human and the screaming, yelling large humans, the owl opened his eyes. He stared down at the coyote for a long moment, then said, "Your curiosity will be the death of you if we don't get you out of the city as soon as possible. Posthaste. Pronto."

Trouble knew in his heart it was true.

Rosebud trembled. "I can show you where that train station is," she said. "I remember it well." Among their many virtues, opossums have excellent memories.

The Professor regarded the sensitive, none-too-brave marsupial. "Are you sure you want to be involved in this escapade? It could prove dangerous."

Rosebud swallowed, then nodded. "Yes," she said. "If it will save Trouble, then yes."

Trouble nuzzled his friend.

"The truck will be back the day after tomorrow, so we must leave tomorrow night," Mischief said. "Until then," he said, glaring at the pup, "I'm not letting you step one paw out of this den."

30

Wanted!

"*Mon Dieu!*" Madame exclaimed. She held the next morning's paper out for Minette to see. A photograph of Trouble leaped across the page. Although the photograph was grainy, there was no mistaking who that was looking back at her with wild eyes and a leg of lamb clutched in his mouth.

"It says your wild friend attacked a child," Madame said. "How could that be?"

Minette's stomach knotted in fear. She knew Trouble would never attack a human, but she did know he was far too curious for his own good. And she also knew that humans were fiercely, irrationally protective of children. Why, if a dog so much as looked sideways at a child, that dog's person would get an endless lecture about safety, leash laws, and the like.

Minette grabbed her leash off the hook by the door, brought it to the poet, and barked. This was bad. Very, very bad. She had to help Trouble. But how?

The headline screamed: **COYOTE ATTACKS CHILD IN CENTRAL PARK!**

"It's all my fault," Amelia groaned. "What was I thinking, trying to feed him?" Although she could hardly bear to do it, she read the article again.

> **As reported in this paper two days ago, a wild coyote has been sighted in Central Park. Now it appears the same coyote attacked a child in the area known as The Ramble yesterday.**

"I'm *not* a child," Amelia muttered.

> **Dave Allison, visiting from Texas, saw the coyote jump on the child, knocking her to the ground. "We got lots of coyotes where I come from. You can't trust them for nothing." Allison managed to chase the coyote away from the girl before it could hurt her.**
>
> **Starting this afternoon, Central Park will be busy celebrating the Full Moon Festival.**

Police caution park visitors and festivalgoers to be on the lookout for the coyote and to keep their children close. Officer Ambrose Vetch of New York City Animal Control and Welfare said, "This coyote has crossed a dangerous line. I will be scouring the park today, and I won't stop until I find him." When asked if the coyote, when captured, will still be taken to the Central Park Zoo, Officer Vetch said, "No, it's attacked a child. We'll have to put it down."

A tear slid down Amelia's cheek and plopped onto Trouble's face. It was all her fault. Somehow, somehow, she had to put things to rights. She had to get the coyote away from the city, but how? How did one smuggle a wild coyote out of Manhattan?

She felt a hand on the top of her head. "What's wrong, darling?"

Amelia's mother's beautiful face hovered above her.

How could she possibly explain? "Nothing, Mom," she mumbled.

Her mother smoothed the hair away from her daughter's face. "Well, I have no classes to teach today, so you and I are going to the Full Moon Festival in the park. Won't that be fun?"

The festival. Central Park would be crawling with

people. How would she ever find the coyote? She'd have to wait.

"I don't really want to go, Mom," Amelia said. What she wanted was to be by herself so she could come up with a plan.

"I promised Madame Reveuse we would all go together, honey."

"Madame Reveuse?"

"Remember, darling, the old French woman two floors up? The one with the poodle?" Amelia's mother poured a cup of tea. "She used to babysit you sometimes when you were very small."

Amelia remembered. The smell of lilac. The taste of lemon biscuits.

Her mother dropped a quick kiss on the top of her daughter's head. "We'll leave at eleven o'clock, so don't wander off."

Officer Ambrose Vetch studied a detailed map of Central Park spread across his desk. He peered at the area on the map labeled The Ramble, so closely the tip of his nose all but touched the paper. As if he could see where Trouble was.

True to his word, Mischief would not let Trouble wander from the den. When the coyote complained of hunger, the fox brought him a fat rat. When he complained of thirst, Rosebud dragged the Frisbee to a leaking sprinkler head, filled it, and dragged it back to the den. When Trouble complained of boredom, the owl thumped him across the nose with his wing and called him a nincompoop.

Rosebud stroked the coyote's throbbing snout with her tiny paws. "Trouble, get some rest. Tonight, we'll be crossing the city with Mischief and the Professor."

The fox lay down next to him. "You'll need all your wits about you, dear."

Trouble sighed. He would miss the small, quiet wisdom of Rosebud, and the tender heart and cinnamon smell of the fox. How could he leave them? And what about Minette? Mischief wouldn't even let him leave the den this morning to find her and say good-bye.

As if he could.

Trouble curled up in misery with his strip of deer hide and fell into a fitful sleep.

His paws and legs twitched as he dreamed of playing a game of keep-away in the meadow with Twist. No matter how fast he ran, the older coyote was always just out of reach.

Then the dream shifted, as dreams do, to Trouble being chased by something unknown and terrible. He heard the voice of the wolf: "There are some things worse than death." He heard the voice of his mother:

"Nothing good comes from Makers." He felt the eyes of Officer Vetch searching for him. He heard the scream of an eagle above, death talons reaching for him.

Trouble jerked awake. He sat up, panting with fear.

"You had quite a dream, poppet," the fox whispered.

Trouble's heart thundered in his chest. "Something very bad is going to happen," he said.

The fox nuzzled his face. "Not if we can help it."

"Where's Mischief and the Professor?"

"Mischief left to check on some last-minute details," the fox said, "and the Professor is keeping watch right outside."

She nodded at the black boot. "Rosebud is resting."

"Soon you'll begin your journey home, my dear," the fox said. "I'm going to just pop out and find you something to eat. You'll need your strength."

Trouble watched the white-tipped tail disappear through the opening. He didn't think he could eat, no matter how delicious a thing she brought back. He could not shake the dream. A sick feeling of dread moved through his body like a dark poison.

31

Convergence

Mischief winged slowly westward across Central Park scouting the best route to take late that night into the city. They would have only a small window of time in which they might travel unseen.

Once a plan had formulated in his quicksilver mind, the crow flew north. He'd just make a quick stop at the Dumpster behind his favorite Chinese restaurant for a bite to eat.

Just as Mischief began his descent, he saw something that almost made him drop from the sky: there below him, lumbering slowly south through traffic, was the fresh-produce truck. THE fresh-produce truck.

"What?" Mischief squawked. "What in the name

of all that's feathered and fine is Trouble's truck doing here? *Now? Today?*"

"No, no, no," he moaned. "The plan is ruined."

With a squawk, he lifted into the sky. If the truck headed back to the country, they were sunk.

But much to Mischief's surprise, the truck turned left, then right. Mischief watched with growing puzzlement as the truck drove south and east, directly toward Central Park.

As Amelia had expected, people filled Central Park. White tents ringed the south end of the Great Lawn. A jazz band played on the steps of Belvedere Castle. A wide circle of people of all types—teenagers, soccer moms, artists, old hippies, not-so-old hippies, business people in button-downs—drummed on their drums. Kites and balloons floated on the summer breeze.

Amelia's mother talked with Madame Reveuse in French as they strolled along the tree-lined boulevard. The poodle seemed more nervous than usual. She nudged Amelia's hand with her wet nose and whined. The girl frowned at the dog's diamond-sparkle pink collar and ridiculous haircut. She moved her hand away. She had a coyote to save.

Officer Vetch drove slowly along Central Park West, cursing New York City traffic under his breath. He desperately needed to park as close to The Ramble as possible. The pressure was on Vetch from city officials to catch the dangerous beast. Having a child-attacking coyote in Central Park was bad for business. And with so many people in the park, who knew what a wild coyote might do?

A spot opened up. Vetch whipped his New York City Animal Control and Welfare truck into the empty space, cutting off another car. The car honked. The driver yelled out his open window.

Vetch hopped out of his truck, put on his New York City Animal Control and Welfare hat, held up his hand, and said, "Official business! Dangerous animal on the loose!" He grabbed his catch pole from the back, pulled his hat down firmly on his head, and trotted off to The Ramble.

Once away from the crowds, Vetch studied the ground. He would have made any Junior Explorer proud with his tracking abilities. It wasn't long before he found Trouble's tracks and barely discernable trail through the forest. Over fallen logs. Through thickets of ivy, around a bench, and finally to the top of a rise. He stopped to catch his breath and admired the view of the wide lake and the city beyond.

A movement caught his eye. There, snagged on a bramble, a tuft of tawny fur waved like a flag in the breeze.

Officer Vetch plucked the fur from the thorns and rubbed it between his fingers. He held it to his nose and sniffed. Coyote. He knew it in his bones.

He looked closer at the wild tangle of honeysuckle, blackberry canes, and ivy forming a kind of hedgerow running all the way down to the lake. And there, just feet away, was an opening. A coyote-size opening. He pulled his hat down on his head and gripped the catch pole.

Had the fox not been carrying an egg up from the cove . . .

and had Rosebud not been sleeping in the black boot . . .

and the owl resting in the sweet gum tree . . .

Had Minette not been on a leash . . .

and Amelia held by the hand . . .

and had Mischief not been watching with excitement as the fresh-produce truck pulled right into Central Park . . .

Had the wind not been blowing Vetch's smell away from Trouble . . .

things might have turned out differently.

32

A Lot Less Trouble

Too late, Trouble saw a dark shadow fall across the opening of the den. Too late, he smelled the moldy-cheese-rotten-potato smell that was Officer Vetch.

Vetch dropped to his knees and thrust the catch pole into the den, followed closely by his predatory eyes.

Trouble yipped in horror. He leaped from one side of the den to the other trying to dodge the noose on the end of the pole.

Rosebud crawled from her bed inside the boot and blinked in confusion.

The noose dropped over the coyote's head.

"Got you!" Vetch cried.

"No!" Rosebud screamed.

Trouble shrieked in panic and wrenched away from the officer. The noose tightened around his neck.

The pup pinned his sizable ears back and crouched low to the ground. His amber eyes darted from one side to the other, looking for a way to escape.

Officer Vetch pulled. Trouble dug his paws into the wet ground and worked his head side to side. With a grunt, the officer pulled the coyote free of his den and out into the meadow.

The coyote shot straight up in the air. He jerked and he twisted and he rolled. But there was a good reason Officer Vetch was known far and wide as the Master of the Catch Pole: once he had an animal in its noose, it never, ever got away.

Trouble snapped and barked and yowled. Never had he been so frightened.

"You're not going to make this easy, are you?" Vetch said. The officer had been prepared for this. After all, a coyote was hardly a stray dog. And Officer Vetch had learned at a young age always to be prepared.

Holding tight to the pole, he reached into his coat pocket and withdrew a small object. He pointed it at the coyote's shoulder. "Nighty-night."

Just as Vetch squeezed the trigger of the tranquilizer gun, he heard a bloodcurdling scream from above. He looked up to see an enormous owl hurtling down on him, talons outstretched.

Trouble felt a sharp sting. His shoulder began to burn. He wondered if he'd just been stung by a hornet. He let out one last, mournful howl.

Awhoooooooooooooooooooooooo . . . wooooo . . .

Trouble's legs wobbled. His amber eyes drooped. His mind grew as dark and still as a moonless night.

Vetch scrambled to his feet. He searched the sky for the owl. With trembling hands, he picked up his hat off the ground and pulled it down on his head.

"Gotta get out of here before that crazy thing comes back," he said, panting.

Trouble felt the strong arms of Officer Vetch lifting him. He gagged at the closeness of his fetid smell.

"Oh no, no, no, no, no!" Rosebud cried in desperation.

For the first time in her life, the opossum forgot she was small and not a bit brave. She hurled herself at the officer's leg and bit down. Hard.

"Ow!" Officer Vetch looked down to see a small opossum attached, rather fiercely by fifty pointy teeth, to his pant leg.

He kicked at Rosebud with the other leg. She bit down harder. "Blast you, you varmint!" he roared, and kicked again. This time, he managed to dislodge the opossum.

Vetch shook his head and straightened his official hat. "Crazy animal," he muttered. He shifted Trouble from one side of his arms to the other.

Then, he heard the bone-chilling hunter's cry of the owl.

The Professor folded his wings and dived mercilessly for the officer's head.

Vetch dashed for the cover of the deep forest. He watched, heart hammering in his chest, as the owl veered off and screamed in frustration.

"This place is crazy," Officer Vetch panted. "Give me bats in brownstones and raccoons in chimneys any day."

At the faraway sound of Vetch's oily voice, Trouble squirmed.

Vetch tightened his hold on the young coyote. "The sooner I get you to my truck, the better. You'll be a lot less trouble when you're dead."

33

Vetch's Plan

Rosebud limped slowly, painfully back to the den. A rib was most likely cracked but her heart utterly broken.

The fox rushed up the hill to meet her.

"What happened?" the fox cried.

"I tried to stop that human from taking Trouble," Rosebud whimpered. "Really, I did."

The fox's whiskers quivered. "You were so brave," she said.

The opossum slumped down in the grass and wrapped her hairless tail around her bruised body. "Yes, but what good did it do?"

Just then, a black form sliced across the blue sky.

Caw! Caw!

Mischief circled once, twice, then landed with a flutter of wings on the grass.

"You're not going to believe this," he crowed. "The truck is right here in the park! It means a change in plans but still, what luck!"

Mischief waited for cheers and hurrahs. None came.

He stiffened. "What's happened?" he asked. "Where's Trouble?"

With growing horror, Mischief listened as Rosebud told the story of Officer Vetch and Trouble.

"No," Mischief moaned. "No, no."

"What do you think he'll do to Trouble?" The fox asked.

In a swirl of feathers and air, the Professor landed on the hedgerow.

Rosebud and Mischief exchanged a look. "He'll take Trouble to the zoo, won't he?" Rosebud asked.

"No!" the fox gasped.

"That's always been his plan," Mischief said.

"The plan has changed," the owl said, his voice filled with grief, his ear tufts flat against his head.

"I heard the human say Trouble will be a lot less . . . well, *trouble* once he's dead."

For once even the crow was speechless.

"No." All eyes turned to Rosebud.

"We cannot, we *will not* let that happen." Her eyes glowed with fierce determination. "Trouble saved my life. Now we have to save his."

She turned to the owl and the crow. "You two go and track down that human. He's carrying Trouble, so he can't be moving too fast."

She turned to the fox. "Do you think you can carry me?"

The fox stood tall on her toes. "Certainly," she said. "But what will we do when we find him?"

Rosebud climbed onto the fox's back. "We'll figure something out."

She clutched a paw full of the fox's fur and prayed to the patron saint of opossums for help.

34

The Patron Saint
of Opossums

Minette froze in her tracks. Her nose quivered as a familiar scent filled her heart. The scent of wild and longing and bone and blood and boundless curiosity.

"Trouble!" she yipped. She lunged on the end of her leash.

"*Mon Dieu!*" Madame cried as the leash pulled free of her hand. "This is most unusual!"

"I'll get her." Before her mother could protest, and before she herself could wonder why she was putting stock in the antics of a poodle, Amelia bolted after the dog.

The girl ran in the direction the poodle's nose

had pointed. At first she didn't see anything. Then she saw, emerging from the far end of The Ramble, almost hidden in shadows and trees, a large man in an official-looking uniform carrying a tawny bundle in his arms. A tawny bundle with big ears and a bushy tail.

"The coyote," Amelia gasped.

"Trouble!" Minette barked.

The sound of Minette's voice pierced the drugged consciousness of the young coyote. He struggled to lift his head. Fear clawed at his spine as he looked into the eyes of his nightmares, the eyes of his future.

He heard the voice of Minette coming closer. With all the strength he possessed, Trouble twisted in the Maker's arms.

"Oh no, you don't." Vetch jerked the catch pole noose tighter around the coyote's neck. Trouble gasped for air.

Screeeeeeeeeeee!

Officer Vetch looked up just as the Professor slammed into his shoulder, knocking him to the ground. Vetch groaned. Blood stained his torn shirt.

Trouble rolled from his arms. Desperately, he shook his head. Still the noose would not let him breathe.

"Be still, Trouble." He felt the tiny paws of Rosebud pulling at the noose.

173

"Hurry!" the fox hissed. "The human is getting up!"

"It. Won't. Budge," Rosebud said, pulling with all her might.

Trouble's legs buckled. Tiny lights like the galaxies of fireflies in the meadow danced before him.

Amelia and Minette rounded the corner. Amelia stopped in her tracks, her mind trying to make sense of an opossum standing on the back of a fox.

But Minette did not stop. She did not hesitate. She shed generations of civility and training. In two bounds she closed the distance between her and Officer Vetch. Just as he stepped toward the strangling coyote, she leaped.

Officer Vetch screamed. In that instant, Amelia understood: the poodle was not saving the man from the coyote; she was saving the coyote from the man.

Caw! Caw!

A large crow circled round and round the prostrate coyote. It was then that Amelia saw the catch pole and noose.

"Oh no!"

Amelia ran to the coyote's side. The fox growled, the red fur rising on her back. The opossum hissed and bared its teeth.

"It's okay," Amelia said gently. "I won't hurt him."

Mischief landed with a flutter and a hop next to the fox. "Let her try," he said.

The fox stepped back warily. Rosebud moved aside.

Amelia ran one hand reverently along the length of the coyote as she worked her other hand under the noose. "I'm sorry I made so much trouble for you," she whispered. She grabbed and pulled.

Ack, gack! Trouble gasped.

Amelia pulled the noose over Trouble's head and hurled the whole, terrible contraption far into the bushes.

Minette nudged Trouble with her snout. "Get up, Trouble. Oh please, get up!"

Trouble staggered to his feet. He swayed as he looked into the faces of Minette, Rosebud, the fox, and Amelia.

"Run," Rosebud said as the voices of humans grew closer. "It's your only chance."

Trouble tried desperately to clear the fog in his head. "I don't think I can make it to the subway train," he said.

"You don't have to," Mischief said. "The truck is here."

"Here?"

"Here," Mischief cawed. "But we must hurry!"

"You!" Officer Vetch roared. He stood, fists clenched, shirt torn, official hat gone. His eyes were black with rage. "You," he said, jabbing his finger in the air at Trouble, "are nothing but trouble!"

175

He looked around wildly for his catch pole. With surprising speed, he grabbed it from the bushes and charged the coyote, swinging the pole above his head.

"Stop!" Amelia jumped in front of the coyote, the fox, the opossum, and the poodle.

Officer Vetch looked from the girl to the unlikely collection of rescuers behind her and back again.

"It was all my fault," she tried to explain, all in a rush. "The coyote didn't bite me down by the lake. I was trying to feed him."

Vetch frowned. "Feeding wildlife is against the law."

"I know, I know." Amelia felt the animals behind her slowly shift away from her. She knew what they were doing. She needed to buy them time.

She took a step closer to the officer. "I'm a lifetime member of the Junior Explorers Club, so if anyone should know the dangers of feeding wildlife, I should."

Vetch leaned to one side, peering around her. Amelia thrust her arms toward the officer. "Here," she said, trying to draw his attention away from the coyote. "Arrest me. I deserve to be locked up, not him."

Amelia knew the second the word "him" escaped her lips, it was a mistake.

Vetch's face darkened with fury and purpose. "Move," he growled.

"Go!" Amelia cried.

"Follow the Professor!" Mischief cawed.

Trouble locked eyes with the girl for the briefest moment, then wheeled and followed the Professor and Minette away from The Ramble and north toward the Great Lawn, the opossum once again riding on the fox.

Vetch let loose a string of words no ten-year-old should hear. "You stupid girl," he sputtered. "Do you realize what you've done?"

"Yes," Amelia whispered.

Officer Vetch grabbed his now not-so-official-looking hat off the ground and jammed it on his head.

He sprinted across the boulevard to his waiting truck, a large crow following above.

35

Bon Voyage

The friends huddled in a cover of low bushes and trees. The owl watched from a sweetgum tree.

"The produce truck is just over there," the Professor said, pointing with his hooked beak. "Not far, really, but between us and it is a plethora of humans."

Trouble still felt sleepy from the tranquilizer dart. He swayed from side to side. "Can't I just curl up here and take a quick nap?"

"No," Rosebud snapped. "You cannot."

"How will he ever get past all those people?" the fox worried.

"I'll take care of it," Minette said. "But we have to move now."

Rosebud slid from the fox's back and looked up at her friend. "It's time to say good-bye, Trouble."

Trouble felt like a fishbone was caught in his throat. His boundless coyote heart broke.

"How can I leave my friends?" he asked as he looked from one dear face to the other. "You have become my family."

Rosebud's ears drooped, but she stood firm. "You must go, Trouble."

Trouble looked up into the sweetgum tree. "Professor? Must I go now?"

The owl nodded. "It is advisable to make haste," he confirmed.

Trouble sighed. He touched noses with each of them in turn. "I'll miss you," he said.

The fox blinked back tears in her golden eyes. "I'll never forget you, poppet."

Trouble leaned down and touched his long, pointy snout to Rosebud's. "I don't know how to ever thank you," he whispered. "You loved me no matter what."

The little opossum stood tall on her hind legs, reached up, and hugged the coyote around the nose.

"You taught me so much," she said. "You showed me I can be brave."

Minette bumped Trouble with her shoulder. "We have to go."

With one last look, Trouble followed the poodle and the owl away from his friends.

Minette stopped at the edge of the Great Lawn. Humans and music and food filled the field. "How am I ever going to sneak a coyote through all those people?" she wondered under her breath.

She looked up at the owl. "How far to the truck?"

The Professor quickly calculated the distance with his keen sight. "Fifty-six point one seconds at a steady trot."

Then it struck her: humans only see what they expect to see. These humans were preoccupied, as always, with their particular world.

She turned to Trouble. "I need you to be a dog," she said.

"You're going to stay next to my side and do everything I do," she continued. "Since I'm taller than you," she explained. "I'll try and angle my body so most of the people won't see you. But those who do must assume we're two loose dogs looking for our owner."

"Ingenious," the owl said with admiration. "And I'll lead you to the truck."

"Let's go," Minette said, "and no howling or yipping or skulking."

And so it was that a poodle and a coyote wove their way around and past hundreds of unsuspecting humans tanning, picnicking, playing Frisbee, and strolling arm in arm on a bright July afternoon.

And had they noticed, had their curiosity been attuned, they would have wondered at the sight of a large owl winging across the sky. In the daylight.

The Professor fluttered down to the top of the fresh-produce truck. At the front of the truck, the human busied himself boxing up corn and tomatoes for a customer.

"All clear," he whistled.

With one long leap, Trouble and Minette jumped through the open door into the back of the truck.

"Please," Trouble said for the millionth time. "Please come with me."

Minette nipped the coyote gently on his ear. "No, my friend, I cannot come. Just as you are Wildborn, I am Cityborn."

"But I will be so lonely without you."

"You have your family and your home in the wild woods. I have Madame Reveuse," she said. "I am her muse, and she is my home. And she must be very worried about me now."

She nuzzled the coyote's sad, sagging ears. "*Bon voyage,*" she whispered. "*Bon voyage.* I shall always remember you."

With that the poodle jumped gracefully from the truck and disappeared into the crowds, leaving a heartbroken coyote behind.

Before Trouble could follow, the owl dropped down to the bed of the truck and spread his great wings wide. "No," he simply said, with a menacing click of his beak.

With a sigh, Trouble took one last, long look at the New York City skyline and the Makers, more Makers than he ever could have imagined, running, walking, laughing, singing, always on their way to somewhere. Then he turned and went to the back of the truck.

Just as he settled down in a dark corner behind the wooden crates, Trouble heard a flap and a *thump*.

"Ow, ow," Mischief said. "I'll never get used to these tin cans." He hopped over to the coyote.

"Is Vetch still looking for me?" Trouble asked anxiously.

"Nah," Mischief said. "He won't be following us. I dropped his car keys down a storm drain."

Trouble relaxed. He was so, so tired.

"I must now bid you adieu," said the familiar voice of the Professor.

Trouble stood and walked to the tailgate of the truck, where the Professor perched. He looked into the great, round eyes of the owl, so much like twin moons.

The owl extended the tip of one long wing. Trouble touched his nose to the Professor's wingtip. "Safe travels, my peripatetic friend," the owl said.

"Thank you," Trouble said.

Just as the owl prepared to take flight, Trouble said, "Professor?"

The owl turned his head around without moving his body, something that never failed to astonish the coyote. "Yes?"

"Please look after Rosebud for me."

Trouble curled up behind a jumble of boxes. Really, he couldn't remember ever feeling so very tired.

Mischief hopped over to the coyote and settled in the crook of his shoulder.

The crow popped a stray blueberry into his mouth. "Did I ever tell you about the time I—" and "Have you heard the one about—"

Between the warmth of the truck and the endless stream of crow stories, Trouble drifted off into a deep sleep. Later, he did not wake when the human loaded the unsold produce back into the truck. He did not wake when the truck engine coughed and grumbled to life.

Instead, he dreamed. He dreamed of his friends and the moonlit glen. He dreamed of home. His real home in the woods, as the truck took him closer, mile by mile, to his family.

36

North Star

Trouble felt a sharp tap, tap, tap on his head. "Wake up!"

Trouble blinked in the dark. He sat up and shook his head. How much time had passed? "Are we here?" he asked.

"Shhh," the crow said. "Listen."

The truck made a terrible grinding, coughing sound. It lurched this way and that until it finally stumbled to a stop.

"That's not good," Mischief muttered.

They heard the human lift the hood of the truck. They heard the human yell and plead and curse.

The back of the truck opened. The crow and the coyote cowered in the corner.

"Dang good-for-nothing hunk of junk," the human muttered. He grabbed a toolbox and stomped out.

"What do we do now?" Trouble asked. "Are we close to home or still in the city?"

Mischief thought this over. "I don't know," he admitted. "Let me go take a look and see if I can figure it out."

Mischief hopped to the end of the truck and flew into the early-evening sky.

Trouble listened and waited.

Finally, he heard a flutter and a thump. "Mischief?" Trouble whispered.

"Yeah, it's me," a dispirited voice answered. A voice that did not sound like Mischief.

Trouble eased from under his hiding place and studied the crow. "What's wrong?" he asked.

Mischief's wings drooped. "Trouble, I have no idea where we are."

"None?" Trouble gasped.

"None. Nada. Zip and zero." Not looking at the disbelieving coyote, the crow said, "I've let you down. And not just you, but your family too."

Trouble smelled the sadness and defeat in Mischief's heart. He nudged the bird gently with his nose. "I couldn't have made it this far without you."

The human slammed the hood of the truck closed and climbed back in. The stowaways heard him say, "Come on, baby." The engine groaned. The engine sputtered. The engine roared to life.

"Yes!" the human and the crow and the coyote cheered.

The engine died.

"No," Mischief croaked.

The human let loose a string of words that almost blistered the bark off the trees.

An evening breeze scurried through the truck, bringing the scent of the wild: moldering earth, sweet grass, the rich aroma of birth and death.

Trouble had had enough. It was time to go home.

"Let's go," he said to the crow.

Without a backward glance, he leaped out of the back of the truck. Silent as the moon, the coyote trotted along the dirt road. His muscles and spirit sang as he picked up speed. Finally, looming just ahead, silhouetted by the moonlight, the forest awaited. With a yip of joy, he bounded off into the woods.

Trouble stopped and listened. Gone was the constant clang and clatter and roar and rumble of the city. He heard wind in the leaves, the high piping of bats, and the tiny rustlings of night in the forest. He heard the beat of his own heart. He felt his muscles relax.

Trouble searched the wind with his nose, looking

for home. Where was the smell of Singing Creek? The perfume of the old apple orchard?

"I'm not sure where I am," he whimpered.

"I'm no help," Mischief sighed.

Trouble looked up into the darkening night sky. And there it was, shining bright, just like it always had: the North Star. Hope flooded Trouble as he remembered Twist's words.

"This way!" Trouble yipped.

They wove their way through the woods following old deer trails and, always, the North Star. They crossed one stream and then another, trotted past and flew above surprised (and slightly alarmed) cows just bedding down for the night.

Finally, Trouble came to a fork in the dirt road they had been traveling along. He looked up at the sky. The North Star stood high in the sky, and right between the two roads.

"Which way now?" Trouble wondered.

He threw back his head, closed his eyes, filled his lungs, and sang a coyote prayer to the rising moon.

37

Coyote Moon

For the first time since Trouble had left home, his song was answered. First his father's low, deep voice, intertwined with his mother's beautiful, heart-broken howls. And then the sweet, perfect song of his sister, reaching as high and wild as the stars.

"This way!" Trouble barked.

They wove their way through the cornfield, past a scarecrow (which gave Trouble a bit of a fright), and to the edge of the forest. Trouble entered the dark woods, the crow always just above him.

They climbed a hill and followed a ridgeline. The stone beneath Trouble's feet and the ledge he easily hopped over reminded him of the time, so long ago in his memory now, when he had earned his name.

Trouble stopped in the moonlight. He called to his family. Before his howl had finished, he heard an answering call.

"This way!"

The crow and the pup plunged back down to the forest. Trouble's nose worked the night air. There. He knew that scent: apples! His heart quickened.

The sound of his family grew closer.

Trouble flew as fast as any bird. Mischief would later tell Rosebud and the fox and the owl that he was quite sure Trouble's feet never touched the ground as his family sang him home.

Then Trouble stopped. There, he heard it as familiar as the sound of his own heartbeat: the wild, ceaseless music of Singing Creek.

He loped with joyful bounds through the woods and burst into the moonlit meadow.

The yipping and howling stopped. Six pairs of amber eyes flashed with surprise.

"Trouble!"

"Twist!" Trouble yipped with utter joy. "Star! Pounce! Swift!"

The young coyotes chased and wrestled and licked one another in happiness. Trouble thought his heart would surely burst, he was so happy, despite the one or two nips on his ears from his father.

"Trouble," his mother called.

The other coyotes moved away from the pup as their mother slowly approached, her black-tipped tail held high. She sniffed the trembling pup from one end to the other and back again.

"I'm not letting you out of my sight for a hundred and one full moons," she growled.

Trouble rolled onto his back, tail tucked between his legs. "Sorry, Mom," he whined.

Trouble's mother trotted over to the old oak tree and looked up at Mischief. "I can never thank you enough," she said.

Mischief shuffled his feathers. "It was nothing, ma'am. No trouble at all."

"Somehow I doubt that," Mother said, glaring at her wayward son. "Nonetheless, the Singing Creek Pack is forever in your debt. If there is anything, *anything*, we can ever do for you, we will.

"You have our word," she said.

"Our word," the coyotes echoed.

And then, the coyotes resumed their joyful reunion.

After a time Trouble saw the crow stretch his wings and look up at the sky. He knew that look.

He trotted over to the tree. "Hey," he called up to Mischief.

Mischief fluttered down to the ground. "Hey yourself," he said. The two friends looked at each other for a long time.

Finally, Trouble said, "I think I'll miss you most of all."

Mischief searched for something suitably smart-alecky to say. Instead, he found the truest thing within him. "I'll miss you too, you crazy coyote."

Nose touched bill.

And with that Mischief rose into the night sky. He circled once, then circled twice above the meadow. "Stay out of trouble, kid!" he cawed.

Trouble watched as the crow rose high above the forest, his black silhouette seeming to brush the face of the moon—the full moon. So many things he had learned from his time in the city: lessons in friendship, bravery, love, forgiveness, belonging, and home. Things he would carry with him for the rest of his life and, one day, teach his own children. Like the crow said, curiosity can take you a long way, but Trouble now knew love brought you home.

Back in the city, in the wild, green heart of that city, a fox and an opossum played in the light of the full moon, watched from above by a particularly clever owl.

Three blocks west, a curious young girl slept in her

moonlit bed, dreaming of coyote eyes.

And that same moon shone through the window where a poet slept and a poodle composed a poem in the moonlight.

> *Coyote Moon*
> *When the wind howls and*
> *the moon shines high in the sky*
> *always, you are there.*

Acknowledgments

Like Trouble, I'm very fortunate to have a pack of friends and family who support me in so many ways.

My agent, Alyssa Eisner Henkin, deserves the Agent of the Decade award for her unflagging patience and optimism.

Huge thanks and coyote yips to my delightful editor, Maria Barbo. She embraced Trouble's story and was every bit as curious as I was to see what was just around the next corner. And to assistant editor Rebecca Aronson, two paws up!

I am so lucky to have these insightful members of the Writing Clan encourage me and give me invaluable feedback: Jean Reagan, Lora Koehler, Chris

Graham, Becky Hall, and Kelley Lindberg. Thank you! I couldn't do this without you!

And many thanks to Emily Adler for opening her home to me and showing me all around Central Park and the wilds of New Jersey.

I couldn't have asked for a better group of folks to work with at HarperCollins. Thanks to copy editors Andrea Curley and Jon Howard for keeping me from looking like an ignoramus. Thanks to Andrew Hutchinson for bringing Trouble to life with his beautiful art, and to designer Andrea Vandergrift for creating a beautiful book. And heartfelt thanks to Katherine Tegen for giving Trouble a home.

Although they don't know me, I want to thank all the wildlife biologists, conservationists, and researchers who are champions of the coyote. I'd particularly like to give a howl-out to Stan Gehrt, Mark Bekoff, Jonathan G. Way, the Urban Coyote Initiative, and the Urban Coyote Research Program. Thanks to Dan Flores for his important and fascinating book *Coyote America*.

Finally, to my husband, Todd, whose love always brings me home.

Critter Notes

━━◥◣◥◤◢━━

Want to know more about coyotes, crows, and opossums? Read on!

Coyotes: An American Original

In 1999, folks in New York City's Central Park encountered a particularly curious sight: a coyote trotting through the park—"wild and unleashed!" according to one area newspaper. The media named him Otis and followed his every move. The coyote was eventually caught and taken to a zoo in Queens. Several years later, another coyote showed up in Central Park (nicknamed Hal by the spellbound media), and in 2010 a female coyote lived for several months in Central Park before being captured.

What in the world are coyotes doing in New York City?

Coyotes have lived in North America, Mexico, and Canada for over a million years. They can be found in every type of environment, from the deserts of Mexico to the mountains of Colorado; from the lush forests of Alabama to the city streets of Chicago. Wherever they are, they're at home.

Like humans, coyotes are extremely adaptable and are experts at surviving. They will eat almost any-thing—rabbits, rodents, birds, grasses, frogs, eggs, fruit, and animals killed by other predators. They're excellent swimmers and very fast on their feet!

As humans have taken over more and more animal habitats, many large predators—wolves, cougars, and grizzlies—are disappearing. That is hardly true of the coyote. Despite hunting, trapping, and other human efforts to decrease the coyote population, they've not only survived, they've thrived. Scientists estimate there are now more coyotes in the United States than there ever have been.

The coyote's range now includes almost every large city in the United States. They're spotted in city parks, cemeteries, and on golf courses. Any sort of green space will do. Coyotes have been seen playing at night in sprinklers in Chicago's famous Wrigley Field. They've been photographed riding trains in Portland, Oregon. And yes, one was chased into an office building elevator in Seattle, Washington, by a crow.

Coyotes are normally active during the day and at night. However, coyotes living in cities have changed their routines to avoid humans. City coyotes have become mostly nocturnal, keeping their activities confined to night. Rather than raising their pups beneath the roots of an old oak tree, city coyotes make dens in (and under) abandoned buildings, inside storm drains, on the edges of golf courses, and under bridges.

As with humans, family is the most important thing to coyotes. A male and female coyote stay together for life. They have pups once a year, usually between mid-February and late March. The size of a litter of pups is determined by how much food is available that year. If food is scarce, they have fewer pups than when food is abundant.

Although coyotes mostly hunt alone, they live in family groups, led by the alpha male and female. The pack will often include one or two offspring from earlier litters (like Twist) who help raise the young. Everyone in the pack helps feed, protect, and educate the pups in all things coyote. Like all families, they play, love, squabble, and learn together.

The coyote is one of the most amazing wildlife

stories in North America. Coyotes have become our hidden neighbors. They're here to stay.

Crows: Einsteins of the Bird World

Like coyotes and humans, crows are adaptable critters. They can be found in just about any country, on any continent in the world.

What makes crows more adaptable than other birds? Their bird brains! They can reason, imagine, set goals, invent, create, and have an uncanny ability to remember.

Crows eat a wide variety of things. This enables them to live in many different types of places. In a given day, a crow might eat worms, grasshoppers, a mouse, nuts, berries, and Chinese takeout.

Most young birds are chased away from the nest by their parents as soon as they can fly. Not so with crows. The young may stay at home for years. They help guard their family territory, build next year's nest, and help raise the next batch of youngsters.

Crows are one of the few species of animals that use tools and manipulate their environment to get what they want. In Japan, crows have been observed setting walnuts in the middle of intersections so that passing cars will crack open the hard shells. When traffic stops, the crows saunter out to the street to eat the nuts. In Minnesota, crows watched ice fishermen pulling up fish through holes in the ice. When the men stepped away from their lines, the crows pulled the lines out of the water and ate the bait and fish right off the hooks.

Like Mischief, crows are known for their playfulness and, well, peskiness. A family in Russia videoed a playful crow using a metal lid to sled down a snow-packed roof. In the wild, crows love to tease wolves, coyotes, and even bears. They can imitate all kinds of sounds: the meow of a cat, a squeaky door, a dog's yelp, the growl of a snowmobile.

The crow is often referred to as the "common crow." But with its keen intelligence and remarkable memory, crows are anything but common!

Opossums: Misunderstood and Unappreciated

Like our friend the Professor said, opossums are widely misunderstood critters.

Opossums and possums are not the same animal. Opossums live only in the United States. Possums live in Australia and the surrounding islands.

Opossums are the only marsupials who make their home in North America. Just like kangaroos, opossum babies live in their mother's pouch. When they are about two months old, they climb out of their mama's pouch and spend much of their time riding on her back. When they are three months old, they strike out on their own. Opossums are solitary creatures and do not live in family groups. They are most active at night.

Like Rosebud, opossums are peaceful animals. They prefer to avoid a fight if at all possible. When cornered, an opossum will hiss, growl, and even snap its fifty teeth. But when the stress of danger becomes too great, an opossum faints in shock. This shock induces a comatose state that can last from forty minutes to four hours! While "dead," the little critter's body is limp, its front feet curl into balls, and drool runs from its mouth. It even produces a smell that is, well, icky.

No matter where you live, there's wildlife all around, going about their lives just like you. To see them, all you have to do is be still, watch, and listen. But don't touch or feed! Wildlife in the city is still just that: wild.

Turn the page for a sneak peek at
Bobbie Pyron's next friendship story.

Piper

I rest my head against the cold window of the Country-Wide bus, watching the world go by. The full moon lights up empty fields. Cornstalks and stubble throw long shadows across the ground. It's pretty and kind of mysterious too.

To tell you the truth, I think I'm the only person on the entire bus who's awake. Well, except for the driver, but I can't see her anyway. Her name tag said Doreen. She seems nice.

Across the aisle, my little brother, Dylan, sleeps with his head in Mama's lap. His red superhero cape is spread across his body. It's just an old red blanket he won't give up without pitching a royal fit, so we pretend it gives him superpowers, especially when his asthma is bad. I can just see the tips of his sneakers peeking out from under the blanket. He has his best friend, Ted the stuffed shark, tucked under his chin.

I gaze back out the window at the headlights of cars ticking by; at the warm yellow porch lights glowing outside of houses in the neighborhoods we pass. Like our old neighborhood and our little house.

Thinking of home reminds me of the things in the backpack by my feet. Inside, along with my Firefly Girls sash, a jacket, and some other stuff, is my favorite book, *My Side of the Mountain*. I could take it out and read it—again—but if I turn on the overhead light, it'll wake Daddy up.

Daddy snores lightly, almost like a purr, in the seat beside me. I lean my head against his arm and feel warm skin through the thin flannel shirt. I can smell his familiar scent of cigarettes and Juicy Fruit gum. And if I rub my nose just a little deeper into the soft flannel, I swear I can smell the salty sea air of home.

I close my eyes. The bus rocks so, so gently as it speeds through the night past farms and fields and towns, houses and neighborhoods, everyone sleeping snug as bugs in their beds.

Since I can't read my book, I decide to run my favorite "imaginary movie" in my head. I'm not the world's best sleeper, especially when I worry, which is pretty much most of the time. So when I can't sleep, I make up movies. My favorite is *Trudeau Family Wins*

Big! In it, we win the lottery and have all the things we've ever wanted: a house on the water and a big boat for Daddy, a fenced-in yard with a dog for me, college for Mama, and a brand-new bicycle for Dylan. And best of all, no worries about paying the bills.

I smile just a tiny bit. My mind latches onto the rhythm of the rocking bus. It whispers in time, over and over, "Maybe, maybe, maybe . . ."

✌ 2 ✌

Baby and Jewel

A small brown dog listens
to the beat of his world
in the chest of a woman
named Jewel.
He watches a raccoon waddle across the grass
in the bright moonlight.
Baby squirms with curiosity.
Is it doggish?
Is it cattish?
Oh! So many things to smell!
To see!
To make friends with!
Jewel stirs.
Baby settles
against her chest

quiet
a good, good dog.
He tucks his head beneath her chin.
Jewel's scent fills every inch
of the little dog
with deep joy.
Baby and Jewel
a pack of two
warm and safe together.

~ 3 ~

Somewhere

"Time to wake up, Piper."

I sit up and blink at the sunlight filling the bus. Outside the windows are tall, tall buildings, rushing traffic, trash pushed up against the sidewalk curbs by the wind. What happened to the moonlit fields? The tidy neighborhoods?

Daddy lifts his Atlanta Braves cap from his head and runs his fingers through his hair.

"You sleep okay, little chicken?" he asks around a yawn.

I yawn too. "I guess. The moon was awful bright."

Everybody's waking up now. They stand and begin gathering their bags, boxes, backpacks, and suitcases from under seats and overhead racks.

Mama gives me a tired smile as she shifts Dylan

from one arm to the other. "Morning, sweetheart." She stretches and tries to smooth her shirt. Her hair is coming loose from its braid.

"Your hair's a mess, Mama," I say. "Let me fix it."

I undo her braid, smooth down her springy hair as best I can, and rebraid it nice and tight.

"Thanks, honey," she says. She scoops Dylan up off the seat and into her arms. Dylan can sleep through anything. Once he slept through a tornado that hit near our street. Never made a sound. Me, I'm not much of a sleeper. I'm like Daddy that way.

Dylan's eyes open. I watch as he slowly comes back to the world. His eyes are the same deep, deep sea blue as Mama's.

"Where are we?" he asks in his croaky little voice.

I look back out the windows. Nothing looks familiar. Nothing looks like anywhere we've been. And we've been a lot of places over the last few months.

I reach out and push the hair out of his eyes. His face is hot and damp. For just a second, I let my fingers rest against his cheek.

"Somewhere," I answer. "We're somewhere."

"Over the rainbow?" Dylan asks. Me and Dylan used to watch *The Wizard of Oz* every Easter when it came on TV, and we can sing every song.

I smile and click my red high-top tennis shoes

three times. "Maybe."

Mama hands me Dylan's SpongeBob backpack, his red superhero cape, and Ted the Shark. I sling my backpack over one shoulder, Dylan's over the other.

We step off the bus. Mama sets Dylan on the ground while she checks to make sure we have everything. Two suitcases and one duffel bag.

I look around and up. I've never seen so many people and so many tall buildings. Even when we stayed with Mama's cousin in Baton Rouge, it wasn't like this.

"Look, Piper!" Dylan grabs my hand and clutches it hard. There, off in the distance, are mountains so high, they look like they've surely punched a hole right through the sky and into heaven. I feel myself light up inside. Ever since I read *My Side of the Mountain*, I've wanted to see the mountains. Be *on* a mountain like Sam Gribley.

I squeeze his hand. Just like Dorothy when she first sees Munchkinland, I say, "Toto, I don't think we're in Kansas anymore."

❧ 4 ❧

A New Day

"Oh Lord, let me get these old bones moving
one more day."
Jewel says this each and every morning
as she stretches her legs
arms
fingers
back.
Baby wags his bit of a tail
and pulls back his lips in a toothy smile
as he does every morning.
A frisky breeze
skitters across the grass, bringing
delicious scents
to Baby's nose.
The sweet smell of rotting leaves.

The bitter smell of acorns.
The musky smell of squirrels.
Squirrels!
Baby runs tight circles
around and around and around Jewel,
yipping with delight.
A brand-new day to see old friends
and make new ones.
A new day to explore the city with Jewel.
Always with Jewel.
What could be better?
Baby does not understand why sometimes
the smell of sadness and confusion
spools from Jewel.
Like now.
Baby twirls and spins
on back legs.
Jewel laughs.
She lifts Baby and kisses the white patch
on the top of his head.
A patch shaped like a snowflake.
"Look, Baby," Jewel says. "Just look at the world."
And Baby does.
Trees, swings, picnic tables, a pond,
wet leaves carpeting the ground and
in the distance

tall buildings
and farther still,
mountains.
Baby licks Jewel's chin and squirms in her arms.
Let's go!